Tangled Up in Mayhem

Also by Merrill Wyatt

Ernestine, Catastrophe Queen
Tangled Up in Luck
Tangled Up in Nonsense

MERRILL WYATT

TANGLED UP IN MAYHEM

Margaret K. McElderry Books

New York London Toronto Sydney New Delhi

MARGARET K. McELDERRY BOOKS
An imprint of Simon & Schuster Children's Publishing Division
1230 Avenue of the Americas, New York, New York 10020
For information about special discounts for bulk purchases, please contact Simon & Schuster Special
Sales at 1-866-506-1949 or business@simonandschuster.com.
The Simon & Schuster Speakers Bureau can bring authors to your live event. For more
information or to book an event, contact the Simon & Schuster Speakers Bureau
at 1-866-248-3049 or visit our website at www.simonspeakers.com.
Interior design by Rebecca Syracuse
The text for this book was set in Chronicle Display.
Manufactured in the United States of America
1023 BVG
First Edition
2 4 6 8 10 9 7 5 3 1
CIP data for this book is available from the Library of Congress.
ISBN 9781665931052
ISBN 9781665931076 (ebook)

To Ann and Jill.
For mostly not being as weird as
Sloan and Amelia's families. Mostly.
And to Aiden for arriving late to the show.

Prologue

An Unwanted Nighttime Ride

Beneath the sparkling stars, the roller-coaster car lurched forward.

Up the half-finished track of the first hill and toward the one-hundred-and-fifty-foot drop on the other side.

Without the rest of the track to catch it.

Thirteen-year-old Amelia jabbed at the release button on her harness, but nothing happened. If she and her friend Sloane could just get out of the car before it started going too quickly, they'd be able to climb over the back and onto the tracks. "My harness is jammed!"

"Mine too!" Sloane cried as the car shivered. The wind off Lake Erie whipped her ponytail around her face. Since the electricity was only turned on for test purposes while it was being built, the roller coaster didn't seem to be working exactly as intended.

Rather than speeding upward, the car's wheels ground against the track, reluctant to begin its trip forward.

Which Amelia could understand.

She was reluctant to begin it too.

And even more reluctant to finish it.

Roller coasters—she'd always known they were a bad idea. Fling people up toward the sky and then smash then back toward the earth again? Then be pleasantly surprised when they didn't end up as gooey messes?

Yeah, seemed like a great idea.

Amelia had always known that, eventually, something could go wrong.

She just had never imagined that it would be someone trying to murder her.

Next to Amelia, Sloane tried to wriggle free from the harness. Unfortunately, test car or not, the harness was there to keep people from falling out.

No matter how badly they wanted to fall out.

To keep from plummeting even further.

As Sloane continued to struggle, Amelia looked down at the murky, gravelly construction site around them.

Icy cold panic gripped her.

This was a nightmare.

She'd had *actual nightmares about this exact thing!*

That was it.

There was no way Amelia's brain was going to let the outside world be as scary as the things in it sometimes were!

"Nopenopenopenopenope!" Amelia shrieked, twisting and contorting her body like a snake.

As already mentioned, harnesses are designed to keep people inside a roller-coaster car, no matter what the laws of gravity and physics throw at them.

They are not, apparently, intended to confine an extremely frantic, extremely determined Amelia.

Writhing, she got her head under one strap, and then tugged the rest of her body free as the car angled upward.

Clutching the back of the car, she slid over it and onto the track, tumbling downward.

"Amelia! Don't leave me!" Sloane yelled. She tried to turn around, but her own harness kept her firmly in place. Darn her strong bones and muscles!

Amelia, however, didn't answer.

Left alone in the roller-coaster car, Sloane faced forward again.

She could see where the tracks gave way to the night sky.

To nothing but empty air.

This couldn't be happening.

This couldn't be how her summer vacation ended.

Best case scenario, she was going to end up in a full body cast in the hospital rather than starting her eighth-grade year with everyone else.

Worst-case scenario . . .

Well, Sloane didn't want to think about the worst-case scenario.

How had they gotten here?

Why had they ever accepted this investigation in the first place?

The end of the tracks loomed closer . . .

. . . and closer.

One

A New Case

It all began—as these things usually did—with Amelia being extremely dramatic.

There was nothing particularly surprising about that. Amelia was usually dramatic.

What *was* unusual was that she was being dramatic at a softball game.

(It should be noted that plenty of people get excited at softball games. However, that's typically because they're watching the game and have strong feelings about how their team is doing.)

However, when Amelia began shouting, it had nothing to do with the game.

In fact, she wasn't even aware that there was a softball game going on at all.

On the other hand, Sloane noticed the game.

Maybe because she was in it.

The sun hit her eyes as she stepped up to bat. She tugged at the brim of her cap and squinted. Overhead, the sun panted in the sky above the Wauseon softball diamonds. As though trying to find a cloud with which to shade itself—and finding none. Puffs of dust rose from the grass in the outfield, which had turned crispy and brown with the July heat. Nearby, a train rumbled along the tracks, shaking loose chunks of gravel and adding even more dust into the air.

On the pitcher's mound, Mackenzie Snyder squinted back at Sloane. She wasn't trying to block out the dazzling sunlight, however.

She was doing it because she didn't like what she was seeing.

Specifically, Sloane.

Shrugging, Sloane hefted her bat onto her shoulder and braced her legs. She knew how Mackenzie pitched. Just a little too close to the batter's body. Not close enough to hit them, just close enough to make a nervous batter flinch backward.

Fortunately, Sloane wasn't nervous.

Her teammates called her "Slayer Sloane" for her killer nerves under pressure.

But as Mackenzie cranked back her pitching arm, Amelia appeared in the far parking lot near the high school, running and shrieking, "Sloane!"

Instinctively, Sloane's head twitched away from Mackenzie and toward her friend. Short and with a fiery mane of red curls, Amelia had made it across the parking lot and now ran along the chain-link fence separating right field from a creek bristling with wildflowers.

"Strike one!" the umpire cried as the softball whizzed past Sloane and was caught by Mackenzie's teammate Kyleigh.

"Aw, Mr. Roth!" Sloane turned toward her seventh-grade English teacher. He made extra money in the summertime by umpiring softball games. "I was distracted!"

"Sorry, Sloane." He crossed his arms. "That's on you. Mac's pitch was perfectly good."

Out on the mound, Mackenzie cackled as Kyleigh slung the ball back to her.

"Sloane! Sloane-Sloane-Sloane!" Amelia tried to climb the chain-link fence. Neither terribly coordinated nor wearing very good shoes for it, she didn't succeed. "Sloane! You won't believe the news!"

News? In spite of herself, Sloane found her attention jerked toward Amelia again. Whatever it was, it probably had to do with their detective agency and YouTube channel: Osburn and Miller-Poe Investigations.

"Mr. Roth, can I please have a second?" Sloane begged, but her teacher-turned-umpire shook his head.

"Sorry, Sloane," he said again. "Not unless your coach calls a time-out."

Over in the shade of the ancient dugout, Sloane's entire team glared at her, daring her to use up one of their precious timeouts.

Sloane swallowed and lifted up her bat, ignoring Amelia's pleas.

Mackenzie smirked at her. In typically evil-but-perfect Mackenzie "Mac Attack" Snyder fashion, she timed her next pitch just right.

Right, that is, as Amelia drew closer, rattling the metal fence and shrieking, "It's amazing! But we have to come up with a plan quick! Before my family does!"

Amelia's family? Sloane shuddered at the thought.

And swung a second too late.

"Strike two!"

Amelia released the fence and disappeared behind the dugout, closer to the gate. Sloane prayed that Mackenzie would pitch before Amelia made it onto the diamond.

Mac did, for once mistiming the exact moment to make someone else miserable.

Grateful that even evil geniuses sometimes mess up, Sloane cracked the ball into the outfield. Mylie, the right fielder, tried to catch it, but her glove just missed. A fraction of an inch higher, and the softball would have made it over the fence and splashed into the creek, guaranteeing a home run. Instead, it chunked against the metal bar and thudded into the weeds.

Sloane would have to run for it.

"RUN!" her coach and teammates screamed from the dugout. "Run, Slayer, run!"

She took off toward first base.

As Amelia burst through the gate.

"Sloane!" Amelia panted behind her friend, completely uninterested in everyone shouting at her to get off the field. "We've been hired! Actually hired! With money! Someone wants to pay us to solve a mystery!"

What? What?! Hitting first base, Sloane's instinct was to turn around. Instead, she forced herself to pivot toward second and pick up the pace.

Lifting up the skirts of a white dress that had no place on a dirty baseball diamond, Amelia chugged along after Sloane, still talking, "He saw the series we did on Ma Yaklin's Missing Millions last month, and he was super impressed!"

"Amelia Miller-Poe, get off the field!" Mr. Roth shouted. When that didn't stop her, he blew his whistle.

In the dugout, half of Sloane's team was chanting "Run, Slayer, run! Run, Slayer, run!"

While the other half yelled at Amelia.

Sloane ignored it all, reaching second base. She wasn't breathing properly and her running form was terrible, thanks to the distractions, but Sloane ignored that, too.

Because out of the corner of her eye, she saw Mylie flee from a hornet guarding the ball.

She could do this. She could make it.

Behind her, an exhausted-but-determined Amelia kept up, even though she lost a white shoe somewhere around second base when her heel broke. "He heard that BuzzFeed might be doing an interview with us and that we might even be getting our own show on Apple TV!"

BuzzFeed? Apple TV? When had all *that* happened? This was all new to Sloane. It was also almost enough to get her to slow down and turn around.

Almost.

But not quite.

Her lungs knocked against her ribs, begging her to stop. Sloane reached third base just as Mylie finally stunned the hornet with a swat of her leather mitt and scooped up the ball. By now, everyone was screaming.

At Sloane to run harder.

At Mylie to throw the ball.

At Amelia to get off the dang field.

"We're actually getting hired, Sloane! By someone who wants to pay us! But my family wants to 'help'! We've got to stop them, Sloane!" Amelia managed to make herself heard over the shrill screech of Mr. Roth's whistle.

The softball zoomed through the air. Sloane put on an extra burst of speed, not caring if her lungs collapsed from the effort. She slid into home plate in a cloud of dirt and flying clumps of dandelions as she heard the *THWACK* of the ball hitting Kyleigh's glove.

"*SAFE!*" Mr. Roth shouted his verdict.

Sloane's team roared their approval as Mackenzie stormed in from the pitcher's mound to argue. Sloane remained on the ground.

Gasping for air like a beached goldfish.

Amelia's sweaty, freckled face and frazzled curls blocked out Sloane's view of the sky above.

"He's in town today from Sandusky and wants to meet us at the Red Rambler Coffee House at three this afternoon. But my parents say we can't meet him there without an adult," Amelia panted, flopping down on the chalk line next to Sloane. Much like the chalk line itself, Amelia's dress was no longer as white as it had once been. "I mean, not just some random adult either, but—you know—one of *our* adults. Now, my mom and dad and Aiden and Ashley are all trying to rearrange their schedules so they can be there. We can't let them, Sloane! Even if they don't take over, they'll creep him out! What are we going to do?".

"Ungh" was all Sloane could come up with. She really needed a drink of water. And to get off the field so the next batter could come up. Without stepping on Sloane's face. Which Taylor from the other team was threatening to do as she came in to replace Mackenzie as pitcher since Mr. Roth kicked her off the field for bad sportsmanship.

"I don't know what 'ungh' means!" Amelia got to her feet, dragging Sloane along with her. Then she froze. "Oh no. They're here."

Amelia's tone dropped from loud and frantic to a soft whisper of horror.

Following her friend's gaze, Sloane watched as a shiny black BMW minivan careened its way into the parking lot, sending gravel skittering everywhere.

A very noisy, very bossy, very confident group of Miller-Poes poured out of it.

They stormed the field as though there to pillage it. There were only four of them, but somehow, there always seemed to be more. A whole pack of Vikings, barking out orders and their opinions.

All while truly believing they were actually helping.

"I'll review the contract details!" Amelia's father, the Judge promised. "See if we can't squeeze a few more dollars out of this fellow!"

"I want terms! And conditions!" her mother, Amanda Miller snapped.

"Don't worry, Amelia! We'll be with you the entire time!" her half brother, Aiden, promised while her half sister, Ashley, nodded vigorously and added, "We'll be your security team!"

With a whimper, Amelia collapsed onto the baseline again. As though trying to camouflage herself there.

Having had all three Miller-Poe children in class over the years, Mr. Roth was used to dealing with the family. He got Amelia to her feet and shoved everyone out the gate to the bleachers.

Free of distractions (aside from the yelling that continued over by the bleachers), the game resumed.

Sloane crawled back to the dugout, where she collapsed in a filthy, sweaty heap onto the bench and chugged water from a paper cone. Her teammates all slapped her approvingly on the back.

However, despite Sloane's run, Mackenzie's team won by one point.

Ugh.

"It's your friend Amelia's fault," one of Sloane's teammates grumbled.

Funny how quickly Sloane had gone from hero to villain.

Or at least the villain's friend.

"*You* missed that fly ball of Kyleigh's," Sloane shot back. The girl grabbed her bag and flounced off without any more complaints about Amelia.

Who had spent the rest of the game on the sidelines, surrounded by her family.

Shouting and arguing among themselves.

While Amelia melted onto the hot, metal bleachers. She was now a puddle of white skirts, red hair, and misery. Chin resting on hand, waiting for her family to tire out.

"I can't go!" The Judge swiped at his phone, nose practically pressed to the screen. "I've got to hear arguments for a search warrant about some sort of shady illegal bingo operation that's going on in town."

"I'm lifeguarding all afternoon at the pool!" Aiden, studied his own phone. "Maybe I could just leave behind a bunch of life preservers?"

"I've got a very important investor lunch!" Amanda Miller cried. "Maybe I could tell them to check out that bingo operation?"

"I have to do filing at the courthouse!" Ashley huffed. "Judge Friedman gets very upset when her nails aren't nice and even!"

Sloane dragged her bag over to her friend on the bleachers. Only to shoot back up again as the blisteringly hot metal touched the bare skin of her legs.

"YEEE-OUCH!" Sloane hopped around, trying to cool them off.

All the Miller-Poes stopped talking and blinked at her in surprise.

Amelia seized the moment of silence. "Remember what our family therapist said? You all need to listen more and stop trying to control everything! Don't make me tell Dr. Spieles on you!"

That set off another round of outraged comments. Miller-Poes did not like being tattled on.

Because it implied that Miller-Poes had done something wrong.

Which, in turn, hinted that they might be less-than-perfect.

And that was obviously a crime.

As Sloane rubbed at her scorched thighs, her gaze fell on her Granny Kitty and Granny Pearl sitting in the grass beneath an elaborate striped-and-tasseled private tent.

"My grannies will do it," Sloane croaked, still thirsty. When no one other than Amelia heard her, Sloane croaked louder. "Hey, *hey.* My grannies can go with us."

Once again, everyone stopped jabbering over each other. They swung their attention toward the striped-and-tasseled tent.

Granny Kitty, Granny Pearl, and Great-Grandma Nanna Tia— sat in its shade. Battery-powered fans added a cooling breeze as Nanna Tia relaxed in a lounge chair. She wore a straw hat, sunglasses, and a loose flowery dress. Sipping a smoothie from a coconut shell, she watched as Granny Kitty and Granny Pearl counted stacks of money.

The two of them wore matching floral tracksuits, running shoes, and fanny packs. They both wore visors on their heads like they had stumbled out of a Las Vegas casino's money-counting room.

Which . . . they sort of had.

Realizing it, Sloane gasped and stormed over to them.

"Are you betting on the games again?" she demanded, causing Granny Kitty to freeze as she licked her fingers to better index the wad of one-dollar bills in her hands.

Granny Kitty exchanged a guilty look with Granny Pearl.

"Erm," Granny Pearl cleared her throat awkwardly. Usually, the grannies weren't at a loss for words. Suddenly suspicious, Sloane snatched up a piece of paper from the table and scanned it.

"You're taking bets *against* my team?" Sloane gasped in outrage. "And you're heavily favoring the *other* team?"

"Wait, what?" The Judge hurried over and reached for the paper. "That isn't legal!"

"Oh my! Isn't it?" Granny Kitty went all fluttery, assuming the persona of a confused, little old lady.

"We had no idea!" Granny Pearl swore.

Over in her lounge chair, Nanna Tia sipped her coconut smoothie and said, "Does your mother-in-law know it's illegal? Because she phoned in a bet from Florida."

This gave the Miller-Poes something new to shout about.

Amelia hooked her friend by her very sweaty, very stinky collar and dragged her into the shade beneath the bleachers. She handed Sloane a Gatorade that she'd fished out of the grannies' cooler. "Maybe they'll all argue long enough that we can meet up with Mr. Collymore on our own."

Sloane wiped the back of her hand across her brow. Her long black ponytail lay wetly against her neck. "Wait. What? Who's Mr. Collymore? Is he from BuzzFeed or Apple TV?"

Mackenzie swaggered past right at that moment. Somehow, in spite of the heat and all the exercise, she looked perfectly cool and collected. While Sloane's hair had wilted beneath her ball cap, Mackenzie's blond ponytail remained annoyingly perky and bouncy.

Hearing Sloane, Mac rolled her eyes and sneered, "Oh please. No one from BuzzFeed or Apple TV would be interested in your weird detective show. Only losers watch your YouTube channel anyhow."

"More than fifty thousand losers!" Amelia objected hotly. "I'll have you know we're number one in Denmark now for historical mysteries hosted by people under the age of eighteen! That's a lot of losers!"

Which . . . admittedly wasn't exactly the best comeback ever.

Still smirking, Mac flounced off.

"*Grrrrr.*" Amelia stomped her foot. "Just once, I'd like to win with her!"

Sloane swept the hat from her head and used it to fan her face. "Forget her. She's just jealous that people from BuzzFeed *and* Apple TV are interested in our channel . . . Amelia? Why are you looking like that, Amelia? There *is* someone from one of those places who's interested in us, right? You didn't just make up this Collymore guy, did you? Amelia, answer me."

Amelia suddenly had the same shifty look the grannies got when Sloane caught them in the middle of a scheme.

Twisting her fingers together nervously, Amelia felt her face flame even hotter than it had from Mackenzie's humiliation. "Well . . . I might have exaggerated a little. Mr. Collymore is some rich guy from Sandusky. His daughter is one of our followers. It's just that—well, with everyone yelling at me, I got all nervous! So, I kind of made it sound more important so they'd get how big of a deal this is. I thought if I said BuzzFeed and Apple TV were interested in us, everyone would stop being mad and get why I was so happy."

"Urk." Sloane got a whiff of how stinky the inside of her cap really was. She stopped fanning herself. "Okay, that's disappointing. But it's also exciting that someone wants to hire us. *If* we can get an adult or two to go with us."

Both girls swung their attention back to the grannies' fancy tent. The Judge was deep in conversation with Nanna Tia. Just like his daughter a moment before, he'd gone red in the face, and was gulping like a goldfish, too. He and Amelia had never actually looked more alike.

"Now, now." Nanna Tia patted the Judge on the arm. "Betting is just a bit of harmless fun. All the money we make is donated to the Fulton County Humane Society to help take care of those poor cats and dogs. Same with our little knitting club!"

This was, in fact, all true. The grannies ran a variety of technically illegal betting clubs. They gave the county's senior citizens something to do, while providing plenty of money to feed, shelter, spay, and neuter unwanted pets.

However, those clubs were still illegal.

"Knitting club?" The Judge looked confused. "I heard it was an illegal bingo club!"

Nanna Tia chuckled indulgently as she led the Judge and the rest of the Miller-Poes toward their shiny black van. "Why don't you come to my house with the police for their surprise visit this afternoon so you can see for yourself. Oh, and don't worry about Amelia! Kitty and Pearl will take care of her."

With that, Nanna Tia shoved the Judge into the passenger seat of the van.

"'Take care of her'?" he squeaked.

"*Good* care of her." Nanna Tia smiled and shut the door.

As the Judge pressed his face against the window—clearly trying to figure out if his daughter would be safer with or without Granny Kitty and Granny Pearl—the rest of the Miller-Poes stuffed themselves into the van.

This included Amelia. Who'd been snagged by her mother so

she could "... change into something more sensible. What on earth *are* you wearing?"

Like her father, Amelia pressed her face against the glass. "Have your grannies pick me up in an hour! And what I said earlier about BuzzFeed and Apple TV is sort of true! I've emailed them both and tagged them in our latest TikToks! So they might interview us or want to set us up with our own reality show! You never know!"

As the van pulled away, neither girl realized that getting a deal with BuzzFeed or Apple TV wouldn't be their biggest problem.

That they'd both soon be riding a roller coaster straight out of a nightmare.

Or that they'd literally become tangled up in mayhem before it was all over.

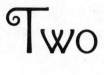

Two

Hired!

The Miller-Poe family lived in a big, sparkly house next to a big, green golf course full of big, sparkly ponds. To Amelia, practically everything about both the house and the golf course screamed, *LOOK AT US!!! AREN'T WE PERFECT AND AMAZING???*

Everything except herself.

(In defense of the Miller-Poes, they didn't intend to scream that at Amelia. The purpose of the big, sparkly house was to scream at everyone else. That's usually the purpose of such houses. To shout other people down. In the case of the Miller-Poes, when the house said, *Look at us! Aren't we perfect and amazing?*, what it was really saying was, *Please don't answer that question!* Being a Miller-Poe involved a lot of anxiety.)

"You know we're very proud of you, right?" Amanda Miller drew the minivan to a screeching halt in the garage. The garage—like the house and golf course—was also big and sparkling in a way a garage had no right to be.

Everyone tumbled out of the van so they could quickly fix themselves lunch before getting back to work. (In the Miller-Poe world, that meant "power" salads made from kale and "power" protein shakes made from even more kale. Amelia was a vegetarian, but that didn't mean she wanted vegetables in her shakes.)

"If you're all proud, then why won't you let me and Sloane meet with Mr. Collymore alone?" Amelia objected grumpily, waving aside the kale shake, Aiden tried to offer her when she went into the kitchen.

"Amelia, it's just common sense not to meet a stranger without your family around to back you up," Aiden explained. He chugged his shake and wiped his mouth with the back of his hand. "Even someplace public. I wouldn't go meet some rando without Ashley to back me up. And you'd do the same, right Ash?"

"Right." With one hand, Ashley stabbed distractedly at a salad. With the other, she tapped at her phone. "How do you know this guy is legit?"

Scowling, Amelia found some hummus and pretzel chips to eat. Everyone else scarfed down their food like it was some sort of competition. Which, with the Miller-Poes, it usually was.

"His name is Covington Collymore the Sixth. He lives in Sandusky, and he wants us to find something that his ancestor, Covington Collymore the First, lost about a hundred years ago. Plus, his daughter is a fan of ours, which is how he first heard about us."

Ashley pulled up the Facebook page for a Covington Collymore VI from Sandusky, Ohio. "That all checks out. Ooo! He's got an amazing mansion on the water!"

She swiveled her phone around so she could show the rest of the Miller-Poes a very modern-looking house overlooking Lake Erie. It had clean glass walls and clean steel roofs, and generally made Amelia feel very grubby and sticky just looking at it.

However, her family was impressed.

"It looks like his daughter is on the same dance team as your classmate Mackenzie Snyder," her mom said, looking closer. "Her name is Carrington Collymore, but it looks like she goes by CeeCee. And the name of their dance team is . . . We Dance Better Than U. Huh. That's a little cocky."

It took a lot for a Miller-Poe to think something was arrogant.

Amelia's heart sank at the mention of Mackenzie. She hadn't known that CeeCee was friends with Mac. How could she be both a fan of Sloane and Amelia's *and* BFFs with their sworn enemy?

Unless she wasn't actually a fan of Sloane and Amelia, and this was somehow all a big joke.

No, it couldn't be that. It just couldn't be. Or, at the very least, Amelia wasn't going to believe it until she had more proof than CeeCee simply being on the same team as Mackenzie.

Maybe the two of them weren't really friends.

Maybe they were just teammates.

Better still, teammates and bitter rivals. Like Sloane and Mackenzie were during volleyball season.

Yes, bitter rivals would be good. Amelia perked up, much preferring this version of Mackenzie and CeeCee's relationship.

In fact, she liked it so well that she gave in to her mom's next request.

"Please. Just . . . let us help? A little?" Amanda Miller asked hesitantly. She didn't normally ask people questions. Normally, she told them what to do. Clearly, *asking* rather than *ordering* took every bit of willpower that she had. She practically strained with the effort of it. Smiling pleadingly, teeth clenched as she squeezed her hands together.

"Oh all right," Amelia agreed hesitantly.

The next thing she knew, Amelia found herself shoved into a black suit identical to her mom's uniform of power suits. (To go along with the power salads and the power shakes. The best way to sell a Miller-Poe anything was to add the word "power" to its name.) Then Amanda Miller twisted Amelia's curls into a tight bun, somehow managing to tame its usual frizz. She jammed pearl earrings into Amelia's lobes, twisted a matching pearl strand around her neck, and thrust a pair of heels onto her feet.

Looking in the mirror, Amelia saw an identical, miniature version of her mother.

It was horrifying.

And yet . . .

Amelia also had to admit that it was the right style for the role she was playing today. She was about to go into an important business meeting. A meeting that could maybe-possibly-someday-eventually turn into an interview with BuzzFeed and a deal with Apple TV.

So Amelia didn't change out of the black suit, and when Sloane pulled up in her grannies' station wagon, Amelia staggered out to it in her heels.

"Wow. You look impressive!" Sloane said encouragingly. For her own part, she was grateful to have showered and changed into a clean pair of leggings and a shirt. That was Sloane's idea of power dressing.

They drove across town to the Red Rambler Coffee Shop near the Walmart. It sat in an elderly strip mall, but it was actually pretty cozy on the inside. Large windows let in lots of golden sunlight, while flowers in vases added blooms of color, reflected in the chrome of the tabletops.

Nanna Tia was off showing both the Judge and the local police department the "knitting club" she ran in her living room. That made Granny Pearl and Granny Kitty more than happy to be chaperoning Sloane and Amelia instead of answering awkward questions asked by people with badges. The grannies ordered caramel frappés and settled down at a table toward the back of the coffee shop.

They both wore sunglasses with their athletic suits, and looked like a pair of elderly mobsters.

Which . . . wasn't entirely wrong.

When Sloane tried to order a caramel frappé too, Amelia stopped her.

"We're serious business people," Amelia explained. "We need to drink serious drinks." To the barista, she said, "Two plain black coffees, please."

"But I don't like plain black coffee!" Sloane protested. "It tastes like shoe polish!"

"You don't know that. You've never had shoe polish!" Amelia accepted the cups and sat down at a table toward the back. "See, this is a power move. By sitting at the back, we make Covington Collymore come to us."

"Sure." Sloane figured Amelia knew better than she did about these things. "Is it a power move to order a chocolate chip cookie?"

"Definitely not."

Sloane sighed. Her stomach rumbled and begged her to ignore her friend. However, Sloane was pretty sure that if she tried to get one of those cookies, Amelia would fling it across the room like a Frisbee.

Sometimes Amelia could be every bit as scary as the rest of her family.

A fancy red sports car zipped into the parking lot off Shoop Avenue. It screeched to a halt in a space close to the coffee shop, and a man of about Sloane's Dad's age hopped out the driver's side. The passenger side door opened too, and a girl climbed out. She wore a tight athletic suit of the kind dancers and cheerleaders frequently wore.

Covington and CeeCee Collymore.

Next to Sloane and Amelia's table, the bathroom door slammed open with so much force that it made the wall shiver.

Both Sloane and Amelia jumped as Mackenzie Snyder popped out of it like some sort of evil jack-in-the-box. Mac's lip curled as she swept her eyes across the two detectives. Looking out the window, she smiled with satisfaction. "Oh good! It looks like my friend CeeCee Collymore is here!"

Amelia made a noise like air leaking out of a balloon.

Oh no.

Mac smoothed her own silver-and-black athletic suit. "I've shown her your TikTok videos, by the way. She thinks they're as hilarious as I do."

Oh no, oh no, oh no.

Amelia suddenly felt lightheaded.

With an unpleasant laugh, Mackenzie sashayed off to join her friend as the Collymores came into the coffee shop.

Scalding hot coffee sloshed against Amelia's fingers. Letting out a yelp, she realized she'd gripped her paper cup so tightly that the liquid inside had spilled over. Snatching up napkins to clean the mess before Covington Collymore spotted them, Amelia said furiously, "Who cares? *We're* the ones who should be laughing, not her! Who cares if CeeCee thinks we're a joke? I bet her dad can tell that we're not! If they hadn't been watching our TikToks, he never would have heard about us!"

"Ugh." Sloane grimaced as she reached forward to help Amelia sop up the coffee with napkins. "You don't think this is all one big joke put together by Mackenzie and CeeCee, do you?"

Amelia stuffed the used napkins under the cushion on a nearby chair and admitted, "I *really* hope not."

Sloane reached nervously for her ponytail and began twisting it around her fingertip.

Mackenzie and CeeCee settled down at a table by the window with some of those delicious-looking chocolate chip cookies. Covington Collymore got a cup of coffee and brought it over to their table.

"Hi, are you Sloane and Amelia?" he asked awkwardly. He carried a briefcase and wore a button-down shirt and a tie. His slacks had been pressed until the straight creases down the front looked like they could be used to slice cheese. On his head, he wore a baseball cap that said Collymore Automotives, which both · Sloane and Amelia assumed was a business he owned. "You look like the people in the video about Ma Yaklin's Missing Millions. I'm Covington Collymore the Sixth."

Amelia jumped to her feet. "Yes! I'm Historical Private Investigator Amelia Miller-Poe, and this is my colleague, Historical Private Investigator Sloane Osburn."

These titles were new to Sloane, but she went with it as she shook Mr. Collymore's hand.

From their nearby table, Granny Pearl lowered her sunglasses to glare at Mr. Collymore "And *we're* Granny Pearl and Granny Kitty. If you have any funny ideas, like trying to kidnap either one of them, we have a very large garden in which to hide your body. It would be excellent fertilizer for the peony bushes we just planted."

Mr. Collymore's mouth dropped open in shock. He took a step backward, clutching his briefcase like he might need it for protection. "I'm not planning on kidnapping anyone, I promise! I'm hoping these two can help me prove that my three-times-great-grandfather had his land stolen from him. It'll make me millions, if they can."

Rather than answering, Granny Pearl slid her sunglasses back up her nose. Both she and Granny Kitty stuck their straws in their mouths and slurped on their caramel frappés in a terrifying sort of way.

Normally, it's hard to drink a Frappuccino in a terrifying sort of way.

But the grannies managed it.

Mr. Collymore took another step backward, still squeezing his briefcase to his chest. He glanced toward CeeCee like he was thinking about grabbing her, running back out to his fancy sports car, and breaking the speed limit between Wauseon and Sandusky.

Sensing they were losing him, Amelia kicked a chair toward

Mr. Collymore. "Ha-ha! *So* funny, Granny Pearl." She slammed a binder onto the table. "Here is a portfolio of all the cases we've solved to date. As you can see, in addition to Ma Yaklin's Missing Millions, we've also found the Cursed Hoäl Jewels, plus several missing tombstones because I guess that's the sort of thing some people care about. Oh! And also Bunny, the local librarian's dog, when he went missing."

"That's Belinda Gomez's dog," Sloane supplied helpfully. "A library patron was angry about his overdue fines and he lured Bunny away with a rib eye steak."

Casting one more uneasy glance at the grannies, Mr. Collymore lowered his briefcase and sat down. He scooched his chair closer to the table. "Was the dog okay?"

"Oh yes!" Amelia nodded her head. "The guy was playing fetch with Bunny in the park when we caught him."

Sloane finished up the story. "Belinda decided not to press charges against him. But I think the guy sort of wishes she had. She rides a motorcycle, and afterward, motorcycle tracks mysteriously appeared up and down the hood of his car. Now, tell us about this case you want us to solve."

"Want to *pay* us to solve," Amelia corrected, wanting to make that part clear.

Mr. Collymore flipped through the binder. He wore the latest Apple watch on his wrist, and a platinum wedding band circled one finger. Sloane didn't know what platinum was but Amelia did. It was more expensive than gold. Between these things and the fancy car out front, excitement quivered in her stomach. He could definitely afford to pay them.

If this wasn't all some sort of joke put together by Mackenzie and CeeCee.

Amelia wasn't ready to rule out that possibility just yet.

Closing the binder, Mr. Collymore pushed it back to Amelia and took a sip of his coffee. "You don't need to convince me. After I saw CeeCee laughing about your TikToks, I went and checked out your YouTube channel. And I was really impressed! I don't really get what she thought was so funny. Not only did they look more professional than what a lot of kids your age do, you really seem to know how to do detective work. I knew you'd be perfect to help me find a time capsule that's gone missing. See, there's a letter in there from my great-great-great-grandfather, and it's very important that I get it back."

"Why?" Amelia asked. "How is that going to make you millions?"

Mr. Collymore looked around like he thought someone might be spying on them. Lowering his voice, he whispered, "Because I'm pretty sure it proves that Cedar Point Amusement Park is built on land stolen from him. If so, I can sue the company for millions of dollars. *Tens* of millions of dollars."

Sloane was about to ask why he didn't just hire an adult detective. Unfortunately, she made the mistake of taking a sip of her plain black coffee. Her throat closed up and absolutely refused to swallow the disgusting stuff.

As Sloane discreetly spit back into her cup, Amelia asked, "Why hire Osburn and Miller-Poe Investigations? There has to be a detective agency closer to Sandusky than us."

"Well—er—you see . . ." Mr. Collymore hemmed and hawed,

drawing renewed interest from the grannies. "It's hidden some-where on the Cedar Point peninsula itself. They aren't exactly enthusiastic about letting anyone search for something that could cost the park millions of dollars. I figure they'd notice an adult pok-ing around, asking questions. A couple of kids . . . hopefully, not so much."

Opening his briefcase, Mr. Collymore brought out a piece of thin, yellowed paper tucked into a plastic sleeve and slid it over to Sloane and Amelia. Through the shiny plastic, they saw an old let-ter, creased and torn. Then fixed with tape that had also eventually grown creased and torn.

> *My Dearest Petunia,*
>
> *The events of 1875 have always weighed heavily upon my mind. Reverend Callender says that the truth will set me free. But I fear that truth cannot be known before my death. Like a ship on Lake Erie, I can feel myself sailing off into my final sunset. I've hidden a box near the land from which I ran my business. When it's found, all will know what really happened. The corner stone on which all lies rest will show itself to be a fake and crumble. Until then—"The great ships sail outward and return, bending and bowing o'er the billowy swells."*
>
> *Your devoted husband,*
>
> *Covington*

Sloane and Amelia looked at each other doubtfully.

"But . . . it doesn't mention anything about anyone stealing his land," Sloane pointed out.

"I know, but my great-great-great-grandmother was sure

that the 'truth' he was hinting about was the fact that Louis Zistel stole his land. Zistel is the man who started Cedar Point back in the 1870s. Petunia was positive that her husband hid the original land deed in that box before he buried it," Mr. Collymore explained eagerly.

Sloane wasn't entirely sure what a "deed" was and was trying to figure out how to ask without looking stupid. The daughter of a judge—and the younger sister of Ashley, who had a summer job at the courthouse—Amelia knew that a deed was a piece of paper saying who legally owned something.

However, she had a different problem with this information.

"Why not just share the deed with people back in 1875, then?" she objected, taking out her phone to photograph the letter. "Or in 1915, even?"

Mr. Collymore shrugged helplessly as she pushed the plastic sleeve back to him. He smoothed an imaginary wrinkle from its glossy surface. "We honestly don't know. My dad always said it was because my great-great-great-grandfather was running for the Sandusky City Council. Cedar Point was already bringing in pretty good business in 1875, so it would have been unpopular for Collymore the First to make a big deal about it and cause problems for the town. Besides, he'd made a fortune building custom cedar cabinets, and it wasn't like he needed the money. I think he thought he'd get even richer by not saying something. Still, he wanted the truth to be known eventually."

Sloane could understand that. There were lots of times she'd kept her mouth shut rather than snitch. Like the time she had to do extra laps at volleyball practice last autumn because Mylee and

Kyleigh had been messing around and accidentally stepped on Coach Godziek's phone, and he thought it was her. Sloane had kept her mouth shut.

But—even months later—she also really wished everyone knew it hadn't really been her.

Amelia, on the other hand, didn't understand. When anyone in her family was upset about something, they complained about it.

Loudly.

However, she wasn't about to say "no" to a case. Even if finding a piece of paper—which was all a deed really was—wasn't nearly as exciting as finding long-lost jewels or millions of dollars in cash.

"The main problem that I see," she said, tapping a finger thoughtfully against her lip, "is that the Cedar Point peninsula is covered by the amusement park. I mean, there are buildings and roller coasters everywhere. Wouldn't the box have been dug up a long time ago? Or had a coaster built over the top of it?"

Mr. Collymore shook his head. "Not necessarily. My grandfather didn't die until 1915. There are a lot of important buildings in the park that date from that time. There's a good chance that he buried the box somewhere near one of those buildings. I think of it like a time capsule. You don't just bury those in some random field or grove of trees. You bury it by an important building. There are lots of those at the park."

Amelia nodded enthusiastically. "Absolutely!"

Sloane made a face, less excited. It didn't seem like much to go on to her.

Still, they needed a new case for their YouTube channel. Their fifty-thousand followers had enjoyed the video Amelia had put together about Bunny the Overdue Library Dog because who online didn't love a good animal video? However, they needed something if they didn't want to start losing people.

This was ... something.

Opening his briefcase again, Mr. Collymore brought out a contract. "If you're interested, here are the terms of our agreement. I'll pay for you and your families to stay at Hotel Breakers for a week to look around the amusement park. I'll also get you platinum passes to the park so you can go in and out as much as you need. If you find the time capsule with the deed inside, you'll get a finder's fee of ten thousand dollars."

Ten thousand ... *dollars*?

Plus platinum passes? Those would get them into Cedar Point as many times as Sloane and Amelia wanted for the rest of the year.

And—and a week in a hotel?

(Admittedly, Sloane was less enthusiastic about that part.)

Amelia had just taken a sip of her coffee. She promptly spat it into a nearby plant. And not just because it tasted dreadful, either.

Straightening up and wiping her mouth with the back of her hand, Amelia realized that everyone was staring at her. Grannies included.

Since there wasn't anything else she could do, Amelia decided to pretend that vomiting on innocent plants was a perfectly normal part of drinking coffee. Briskly she said, "Obviously, we'll need to look through the contract before we sign. And talk to our families. But ... if everything works out, when would you need us to get started?"

"Tomorrow." Mr. Collymore snapped his briefcase shut and stood up. "If your parents need to FaceTime with me, let me know. Or you can reach me by text, too. Right now, I need to get CeeCee and one of your friends, Mackenzie, to dance practice. They're both part of the same team, you know!"

Sloane and Amelia smiled weakly. As Mr. Collymore walked to the front of the coffee shop, CeeCee and Mackenzie both threw contemptuous looks at Sloane and Amelia. Mackenzie whispered something to CeeCee.

CeeCee laughed like it was the funniest thing she'd ever heard.

Sloane stared back coolly, but Amelia turned beet red, tears springing into her eyes.

She just knew they'd made a joke about her. She just knew it.

Granny Kitty went and got them both chocolate chip cookies the size of plates as CeeCee and Mackenzie left with Mr. Collymore. She plopped the cookies onto the table, along with mocha frappés that actually tasted good.

Granny Pearl patted Amelia's hand. "Don't you worry about those two, Amelia. They're just jealous. Once you solve this case and post about it on YouTube, BuzzFeed and Apple TV really will be emailing you."

"But how are we going to stay at the Breakers for a full week?" Amelia asked miserably, cupping her drink in her hands. "My parents can't do it this time, and I bet Sloane's dad can't either. He's probably too busy shoving metal wires into kids' mouths!"

Sloane's dad was an orthodontist. So that was actually a normal thing for him to do.

"Oh, that's no problem!" Granny Kitty said perkily. "Pearl and I can go with you! I haven't been to Cedar Point in years, but I hear they have some very lovely flowers there!"

"NO!" Sloane gripped the table to keep from springing to her feet. Realizing that everyone in the Red Rambler was staring at her, including the baristas, she settled back into her seat. Lowering her voice, she hissed, "I mean, yes. But also, no! Yes, that would be super nice of you to go with us. But don't you dare dig up any of the gardens at Cedar Point. You'll get us kicked out!"

Amelia nodded her head vigorously. "Granny Kitty and Granny Pearl, you're both great. But you *can't* steal anything. *Or* talk other people into stealing it for you!"

Both girls had solid reasons to suspect the grannies for this. In addition to running illegal betting rings, they were members of the Wauseon Garden Club.

And the way they gardened tended to be illegal too.

The two grannies assumed an air of complete innocence. Granny Kitty pinched Sloane's cheek, while Granny Pearl pinched Amelia's.

"Who *us*?" Granny Kitty said in a small, wavering voice quite unlike her regular voice.

"Why, we wouldn't hurt a fly!" Granny Pearl swore.

"Hm." Sloane and Amelia both crossed their arms skeptically.

They were right to be doubtful.

Plenty of illegal events would occur at Cedar Point.

Many of them would cause all sorts of problems for Sloane and Amelia.

The grannies just wouldn't be to blame for most of them.

Three

A Little Friendly Competition

This wasn't the first time that Sloane and Amelia had investigated a case away from home.

However, this time, Sloane had a lot fewer misgivings about staying overnight than she had last time. For starters, since Granny Kitty and Granny Pearl were coming along, Sloane felt like she would sorta be taking part of home with her. Also, Sloane packed an entire suitcase with the pillows, sheets, and blankets from her bed. That way, she could pretend to be back in her own room when it was time to sleep. She still had anxiety about leaving home, but this time, it felt manageable. Partly because of the blankets and the grannies.

And partly because the Seife kids were coming along, too.

Cynthia Seife was Sloane's dad's girlfriend. Sloane's mom had died a few years ago, and Cynthia had divorced her husband around the same time. Cynthia had two kids: four-year-old Skye and seven-year-old Brighton. There's nothing quite like having an over-confident four-year-old around to make a thirteen-year-old more courageous.

Most people want to feel braver than someone who rocked out to "Baby Shark" every chance they got.

If Sloane felt only the *teensiest* bit nervous, Amelia's insides positively squirmed with excitement. The Miller-Poe family had taken the girls to investigate their last big case, Ma Yaklin's Missing Millions. This would be Amelia's first time completely away from her family. She'd never even stayed the night at a friend's house before, having never actually *had* a friend until she and Sloane solved their first case together only two months ago.

For the first time ever, Amelia would be free of her family's well-meaning advice.

And not-so-well-meaning judginess.

She was determined to make every minute count.

When Granny Kitty pulled her station wagon into the driveway of the Miller-Poe's big, sparkly house, Amelia lounged on top of an antique steamer trunk. She wore a long, frilly, pale blue dress and white gloves. Over one shoulder, she had slung a lace parasol. (Which is like an umbrella, only to keep off the sun instead of the rain.)

"Tallyho! I declare, I'm ever so chuffed to be traveling in your perambulator!" she trilled for the benefit of her phone, which was set up on a tripod a few feet away. Amelia had started off in an upper-class English accent—or at least her version of it. However, by the time she reached "perambulator," she'd wavered from English to Southern American to Wild-West-cowboy-in-a-movie.

"You know a perambulator is an old-fashioned type of baby carriage, don't you?" Granny Pearl asked as she and Granny Kitty shoved the steamer trunk into the cargo hold of their station wagon.

Amelia had not, in fact, known that.

She'd thought it was an old-timey sort of car.

"Eh, I'll dub over it when I edit our next episode." Amelia squeezed into the back seat of the car. Sloane was jammed against the door on the extreme other side of the seat, with the two Seife kids and their booster seats in between her and Amelia.

Sloane looked sour.

Sour like someone who had just sucked down an entire packet of Warheads and was trying to hide it.

Skye and Brighton Seife were potential stepsiblings of Sloane's. An only child, Sloane understandably had mixed feelings about suddenly becoming a big sister at the age of thirteen.

Not that she hated Skye and Brighton. It was just that they were—well—sticky, stinky, semi-glittery, and *always there.*

Both the Seife kids turned their heads to stare at Amelia as she wriggled into the station wagon's crowded back seat.

"Hi," Brighton said before turning his attention back to Pokémon on his tablet. He had a shaggy head of light brown hair and the air of someone who hadn't yet decided if he wanted to be in the car.

"I like your dress," Skye mumbled from around a drinking straw. She had light brown hair too and wore a sparkly dress with sparkly sandals. "Are you a princess?"

No one had ever accused Amelia of being a princess before in her life.

She preened happily, confiding, "Only sometimes."

Skye nodded solemnly. "Me too."

Sloane stuck her head forward so she could see Amelia from around the Seife kids.

"Cynthia has to be out of town for the rest of this week, and my grannies had already agreed to watch Skye and Brighton," Sloane explained. Her strained smile showed that she was trying very hard to be positive about this. Normally, she could stretch her legs out in any direction she wanted. And spread her snacks, drinks, phone, and books all across the back seat.

Instead, with the Seifes there, her knees were jammed into the back of Granny Kitty's seat. And her books were jammed *under* it, so she couldn't reach them. Brighton had swiped her bag of Hot Cheetos to munch on, while Skye was happily sucking down the s'more frappé Sloane had gotten from the Red Rambler.

This was *not* how Sloane was used to traveling.

"You're so pretty," Skye told Amelia, the Frappuccino's straw still clenched in her teeth. "You should be a movie star. A princess movie star."

Amelia looked from Skye to Sloane and said, "Sounds good to me."

Skye wiggled her feet happily and waved Sloane's frappé at Amelia. "Want some? It's really good!"

The top of the straw was crumbled and wilted from being chewed on. Preschooler slime gooped it up. When Amelia declined, Skye handed the drink back to Sloane.

Who took it with a sigh.

Along with the bag of Cheetos that Brighton had reduced to orange dust.

She wondered if this was just what it was going to be like from now on.

All her things drooled on or chewed up by feral children.

With everyone seat belted into place, Granny Kitty took off toward Sandusky.

Cedar Point was one of the biggest, most popular amusement parks in the world. It sat at the end of a long, skinny peninsula thrust into Lake Erie to race along the mainland. Little more than a narrow pile of rocks at the end closest to the shore, it widened as it stretched out into the water. Giving space for its dozens of roller coasters and rides to soar up into the air.

It took about two hours to get there from Wauseon. Skye got more and more excited as they went. Even Brighton lifted his orange, Cheeto-smeared face up from his tablet and its Poké Balls as Granny Kitty turned the station wagon onto Cedar Point Drive.

Roller-coaster hills and loops rose up out of the foam like the multicolored coils of a lake monster. Seagulls swooped down from the puffy clouds above to feast on funnel cakes and corn dogs plucked from the garbage cans. Cars filled the parking lot, spewing out teenagers excitedly taking selfies, and families with wagons filled with kids. The sun already sizzled, promising plenty of heat— softened by the wind skimming across the water from Canada.

Granny Kitty eased the station wagon along the road, passing by the many roller coasters, an elderly lighthouse made of stone, and the waterpark, Cedar Shores. Finally, they reached the Breakers Hotel, an enormous building, five stories high and very pale in color. In the center, a wide octagonal tower rose upward with wings spinning off on either side, each with a long, sloping roof. Beyond, a yellow ribbon of sand separated the shore from the cold waters of Lake Erie.

Getting out of the station wagon, Sloane tilted her head

upward. "I'd rather not end up hanging from *that* roof. Not this time."

Normally, most people can assume they won't end up dangling from a building.

Sloane used to be that way as well.

Until she found herself dangling from a gutter during their last case.

Amelia wiggled out of the car too, less graceful than her friend. "Don't worry! We're looking for something buried! We probably need to worry more about ending up getting shoved into a hole than chased out onto that roof."

"I'd rather not do that either," Sloane said fervently.

She was dressed the way most people dressed for a day at Cedar Point: tank top, shorts, and comfortable shoes. Amelia shook out her long, frilly dress, tugged on her white gloves, and snapped open her parasol. Striking a pose, she said, "Do I look like I'm from the year 1875?"

"Sure." Sloane figured that was a safer answer than the more-honest answer of "kinda."

Together, they helped the grannies unload the heavier items from the cargo hold.

Not only did this include Amelia's trunk . . .

. . . it also included a concrete goose.

Of the type normally found in gardens.

"Be careful with Bertram Cordelia!" Skye clasped her hands together anxiously.

"Her name is just Cordelia," Sloane gritted back through clenched teeth.

Skye crossed her arms. "It's called a compromise, Sloane. I call her Bertram, you call her Cordelia, and together we call her Bertram Cordelia."

Sloane started to point out that the concrete goose was *hers*, not Skye's. She'd bought it when she needed to bribe someone during her first case with Amelia. However, Amelia kicked Sloane's shin, reminding her that arguing with a four-year-old was not exactly something a mature thirteen-year-old nicknamed "Slayer" should do.

As soon as they settled the goose in a red wagon, Skye hugged it and started dressing it in a sundress, sunglasses, and floppy hat.

"Cordelia prefers her Fourth Doctor from *Doctor Who* costume," Sloane grumbled to Amelia.

She wasn't used to having to compromise. Sure, she had to do it as a member of the volleyball and softball teams. And at school and stuff like that. Everyone had to learn how to compromise there.

However, at home, Sloane had never had anyone messing with her things before. But Skye absolutely loved the concrete goose to such an extent that it was now her favorite toy.

So Sloane would have felt really mean if she didn't share Cordelia with Skye.

But she still *really* wanted to tell Skye to knock it off and leave the goose alone.

Amelia remained oblivious to all these unhappy thoughts running through Sloane's head. She was just thrilled to get a break from her exhausting family. Taking out her tablet, she pulled up the research she and Sloane had managed to put together yesterday after their meeting.

Neither one of them had realized how old the Cedar Point Amusement Park actually was before they went to the Wauseon Public Library and asked the children and young adult librarian, Belinda Gomez, for help researching the park's history and that guy, Louis Zistel, that Collymore accused of stealing his something-great-grandfather's land. Zistel was a German immigrant, and back in 1870, he opened up something called a bathhouse on the peninsula. This made Sloane and Amelia imagine lots of people out in the water with towels wrapped around their bodies as they scrubbed at their armpits with bars of soap. However, Belinda Gomez had explained that, no, bathhouses were places where people could pay to change into bathing suits before wading out into the water.

Then she'd shown them some pictures.

Bathing suits in the 1870s had looked a lot like what Sloane and Amelia wore when sledding in the middle of winter: hats, thick leggings, and puffy suits

In fact, swimmers/bathers wore so much clothing that Sloane was surprised that they didn't sink right to the bottom of Lake Erie from the weight of it all.

Regardless, the place was a success. Zistel soon added a ballroom for dancing and something called a beer garden. Which . . . weird.

The first roller coaster wasn't actually built until the 1890s, so Sloane honestly didn't even know what would be the point of going to Cedar Point until then.

Several buildings on the peninsula were dated before 1915, so

Covington Collymore I could have buried his time capsule with the deed inside near any one of them. For starters, there was the Coliseum. The Pagoda Gift Shop. The Convention Center. The Eerie Estate.

And the Breakers Hotel right in front of them.

"That hotel looks old enough to be haunted." Brighton Seife shaded his eyes so he could look it up and down. It was the first thing he'd said during the entire trip. (Well, other than "Can I have some of your Cheetos?") "Is it haunted?"

"No," Sloane said at the same time that Amelia said, "Definitely."

Brighton looked questioningly from one of them to the other, freezing just as he'd started to get out of the station wagon. Sloane kicked Amelia's shin. Prompting her to hastily add, "But I'm sure they're friendly ghosts! And besides, the worst of them, Maniac McGee, only haunts the shore, not the hotel. Because he drowned while escaping from the Sandusky County Jail and . . ."

Amelia trailed off awkwardly, realizing she wasn't making things better.

The older of the two Seife's climbed back into the car and re-buckled his seat belt. "I'm *not* going in there!"

Sloane tried to reason with him, "But you're more likely to run into Maniac McGee outside. That ghost has never been spotted inside the hotel. Besides, he drowned all the way back in the 1800s according to the book Belinda Gomez showed us. So he's an old ghost. He's probably nice like Granny Kitty and Granny Pearl."

Brighton didn't exactly look convinced. Of the two Seife kids, he annoyed Sloane less than Skye. Mostly because he spent all his time with his nose buried in his Pokémon game. It suddenly occurred to Sloane that she didn't really know much about Brighton. She hadn't even known that he was afraid of ghosts. Of course, who wasn't afraid of ghosts?

But still.

It was entirely possible that Sloane was going to end up being Brighton's big stepsister. Not definitely. But definitely maybe.

Shouldn't she know something about him by now?

As Sloane worried, a sleek black tour bus sped through the parking lot. It looked like something a rock star traveled around in—and like a rock star, the driver seemed to think that everyone else should get out of the way. Skye had been sitting on the curb of a small, ornamental flower garden with Bertram Cordelia, waiting for Sloane and Amelia to drag Brighton out of the car.

She stood up to get a better look at the glamorous bus . . .

. . . only to have Granny Kitty yank her backward to keep the little girl's toes from becoming road smears.

Amelia had turned around too, to see what was going on.

The whoosh of air from the passing bus knocked her into a patch of blue rosebushes.

Deciding that anything Amelia did, she should do too, Skye wriggled free from Granny Kitty and hurled herself in afterward.

Petals flew into the air like confetti.

The rock star tour bus squealed to a halt. Its door smashed open and girls in tight, black-and-silver athletic suits poured out of it.

As Amelia tried to tug herself free from the thorns trapping her in the bushes, she lifted up her head to see what was going on. Swirly silver-and-gold letters on the side of the bus read: We Dance Better Than U Dance Team.

"Oh no." Amelia flopped back into the bushes and played dead.

"Why do I smell sulfur?" Brighton asked, peering out of the station wagon in confusion.

To which, Granny Pearl sighed. "Tootie."

"Tootie" was another nickname for Mackenzie "Mac Attack" Snyder. No one called her Tootie anymore, but when she was a toddler, that had been her nickname due to her enormous farts.

Farts that tended to smell like sulfur.

Mackenzie glared at Brighton as she climbed out of the tour bus. It was the sort of glare that warned she was packing plenty of sarcasm and mean-girl attitude. And that she was not afraid to use either. "That was *not* me."

"Sure." Brighton retreated once more into the station wagon. Like a turtle back into its shell when faced with a predator. Sloane wondered if she should crawl back into the car to comfort him. Or maybe shove Mackenzie into Lake Erie?

Would that be good big-sister behavior? Or bad?

Sloane had no idea. Maybe she should ask Amelia what Aiden and Ashley would do?

And then do the opposite of it?

While Sloane worried about this, a smirking CeeCee Collymore joined Mackenzie.

Sloane scowled and crossed her arms. "What are you doing here?"

"Dance competition, duh." CeeCee sneered.

Mackenzie added, "So, you know, for a reason that's actually going to look amazing on TikTok. Not to make everyone laugh at us like you two losers."

With that, Mackenzie and CeeCee linked arms and pushed past Sloane.

As they did so, Mackenzie jabbed her elbow into Sloane's ribs.

Knocking her into the garden as well.

At least Sloane didn't completely lose her balance like Amelia had. She didn't end up on her butt or covered in thorns. Still, she had to wave her arms about, one leg stuck out in the air, while she went, "WHOA!"

Much to the amusement of the entire We Dance Better Than U dance team.

A woman with sleek silver hair climbed out of the bus's driver seat and joined the dancers. Like them, she wore a black-and-silver athletic suit, though she'd added a pair of crystal-studded sunglasses to her face.

She had a smirk identical to Mackenzie's.

Grandma Millie Snyder.

"Tut-tut!" She snickered. "If you don't have better reflexes than that, Sloane, it's no wonder you're on a losing softball team." With that, all of them strutted toward the front doors of the Breakers Hotel.

Leaving the rock star bus blocking the lane out of the parking lot.

"That was one game!" Sloane protested. "We're second in the league, you know!"

"Now, now, Sloane-y," Granny Kitty soothed as she pried Amelia free from the blue rosebushes. "Just take the high road like we will."

"That's right," Granny Pearl agreed, luring Brighton from the station wagon by promising him there were Poké Balls inside the hotel. "We'll take the high road and bribe someone to sneak a dead fish into the Snyder's room. There should be some on the beach."

While Sloane wasn't entirely sure what it meant to "take the high road," she was *100 percent* positive that it didn't involve dead fish in any way.

A scratched and bleeding Amelia scowled and tried to regain her dignity. Her dress had less lace on it than when she'd gone in. But her curls had more blue petals stuck in them.

However, when Amelia looked at Sloane, she spotted a bigger problem.

"Sloane, where's your phone? I don't see it sticking out of your back pocket anymore."

A frantic search of the flower bed turned up nothing. Sloane and Amelia looked at each other, groaning, "Mackenzie!"

Everyone marched into the hotel. The grannies to check everyone in, while Sloane and Amelia found Mackenzie by the elevators and demanded the phone she'd taken. Of course, Mac swore she only picked it up from the ground and had absolutely *no idea* who it could belong to and was *totally* going to turn it in to the hotel's lost and found.

"Such a good citizen!" Grandma Snyder cooed approvingly and pushed their suitcases into the elevator.

"Have a good time investigating my dad's stupid time capsule." CeeCee smirked.

"Yeah, hope nothing else goes wrong." Mackenzie giggled.

"Like, nothing that could get posted to TikTok," CeeCee added.

They looked at each other.

Then burst out laughing.

"Girls, girls, girls." From the elevator, Grandma Snyder shook her head with obviously fake disapproval. Mac and CeeCee joined her in the elevator.

And gave Sloane and Amelia evil little finger waves as the doors slid shut.

Once again leaving behind the smell of sulfur.

Brimstone, too.

"Sloane, you don't think they're really going to find a way to wreck our investigation, do you?" Amelia whimpered. Then she glanced down sadly at her ruined dress. "Other than this?"

Sloane didn't answer.

She didn't need to. Amelia knew the answer as well as Sloane did.

If Mac and CeeCee had anything to say about it, this wouldn't be the case that landed Osburn and Miller-Poe Investigations a deal with anyone, let alone BuzzFeed or Apple TV.

It would be the case that humiliated them around the world.

Four

Digging Up Trouble

The Breakers Hotel—or the Hotel Breakers, as it was officially called—was built in 1905. It had been updated, fixed, and changed several times since then. Still, walking inside is like drifting backward in time. The ceiling of the lobby whooshed upward five stories to a domed roof. White railed balconies surrounded the octagon created by the empty air. A polished floor mimicked the shape, created by strips of wood varnished different colors. Retired carousel horses watched visitors check in and out.

Possibly haunted carousel horses.

Like much of Cedar Point, the Breakers Hotel is rumored to be haunted.

Ghosts are rumored to still dance in the ballrooms in the quiet of the night.

While another ghost supposedly enjoys nudging people a *little* too close to those balcony railings. If a person believes in that sort of thing.

Not that the average ghost bothers to ask before giving people a poke.

"Are we in room one-sixty-nine?" Amelia asked hopefully as the grannies and the Seifes joined her and Sloane. To Brighton, she explained, "That's the only guest room with a ghost."

"No, we're on the fourth floor." Granny Pearl herded everyone into the elevator.

"Covington Collymore booked us the presidential suite," Granny Kitty said, impressed in spite of herself.

Brighton didn't look happy. He hugged a tasseled fleece blanket to his chest, and he'd stopped looking for Poké Balls. "Yeah, but can that Maniac McGee make it up there? What if he can, *and* he has a chain saw?"

"Why would he have a chain saw?" Sloane asked.

"He's a ghost named 'Maniac.' Why *wouldn't* he have a chain saw?"

He had a point.

Still, Sloane tried to make him feel better. That was what big sisters did too, right? "Because, even if ghosts are real, they'd only have the things they had when they died. Maniac McGee drowned back in 1875. So, the most he's going to have is a boat. Which wouldn't get him to the fourth floor."

Skye piped up, "Yeah, and if that Maniac ghost shows up, Amelia and I will beat him up for you, Bri! Bam! Bam! Bam!"

She demonstrated on a stuffed unicorn that had been riding in the wagon with Bertram Cordelia.

"Yeah, and I'll help too!" Sloane agreed. She might not know much about being a big sister, but she was positive that if a ghost showed up, she should protect younger kids from it.

"That's okay." Brighton turned away. "Skye and I can take care of ourselves, if that Maniac guy shows up."

"Oh." Sloane blinked. "Um, okay."

Embarrassed heat rushed to Sloane's face as she reached for the comfort of her ponytail. She'd been rejected by a seven-year-old! One who would rather face a scary, chain-saw-wielding ghost *without* her help! Sloane didn't know why that hurt so much.

But it did.

Like his words had somehow crawled into her stomach to scrape around in there.

Cutting her.

Couldn't Brighton see how hard she was trying? Okay, sure. Maybe she had only been trying for the last two hours, but still.

Didn't that count for something?

The elevator reached the top floor and everyone got out. Granny Pearl opened the door to the presidential suite, revealing not just the pair of bedrooms that everyone had expected.

Rather, they stepped into an entire apartment of rooms.

The suite had a living room and a kitchen, along with two bed-rooms, each with two king-sized beds. It was mostly white but splashed with carnival colors that matched the artistic photos of the rides hung up in every room. Enormous windows looked out onto the park, the red and yellow of the roller coasters slashing zig-zaggy lines against the blue of the lake and sky.

The grannies claimed one bedroom, meaning the four kids would have to share the other.

"But—but—we need our privacy!" Amelia gasped. She stood in the middle of the living room, still wearing her torn dress and cov-ered in scratches. Sloane nodded vigorously in agreement as she spotted Brighton and Skye bouncing on the beds in the other room.

"So do we," Granny Kitty said firmly.

"Sorry, Sloane-y." Granny Pearl pinched Sloane's cheek. "We're more than happy to help. But the two bed wetters are yours."

Great, Sloane thought, lugging her bag into the bedroom. The blankets she'd brought wouldn't fit on a king size bed. Trying to make the best of it, she announced to the younger kids, "Looks like we're roomies!"

"I guess." Brighton shrugged, and went back to checking out the TV channels.

"Yay! And Amelia too!" Skye clapped her hands together and jumped off the bed.

Double great. Sloane glumly dropped her bag onto the other bed. She wondered if this was going to be her future if her dad married Cynthia. Stuck in a house with two kids who didn't like her? Well, Skye liked Sloane okay. She just liked Amelia better.

What *was* it with Brighton? Sloane tried to remember if she'd glared at him when he claimed her Cheetos. Maybe a little? But definitely not much.

Discretely, Sloane gave her armpits a sniff because maybe she was stinky?

No, she smelled fine.

Ugh. Whatever. Sloane didn't care! If her dad and Cynthia got married, Brighton could be quiet and unfriendly and that would be just *fine.*

She'd have her hands full keeping Skye out her things anyway.

While Amelia changed out of her ruined dress and pulled thorns from her hair, Sloane marched into the living room and sat down on the couch. She looked over their notes again. Wherever

Covington Collymore I had buried his time capsule with the deed inside, it was probably someplace that had symbolic meaning to him. Someplace that represented the wrong Louis Zistel had done to Collymore in stealing his land.

The Breakers Hotel had a good chance of being that place. It had been on the peninsula in 1915, and people would come to stay at it so they could visit a theme park built on Collymore's land. Heck, for all Sloane and Amelia knew, the Breakers Hotel could have been built *right on* Collymore's cabinet-building workshop.

Still, they could easily search its grounds in the evening or early morning when Cedar Point Amusement Park itself was closed. Right now, Sloane and Amelia had agreed that they should start with the buildings *inside* the park. In order of the likelihood that the time capsule was buried near one of them, they were:

> *The Eerie Estate, which had been built in the early 1900s and used to be offices (if fancy ones) for the people who ran Cedar Point. A guy named Boeckling had once lived there, and he had owned the park in 1915.*
>
> *The Coliseum, which had been at the center of the park for well-over a hundred years. It was also the most eye-catching, having towers, domes, and balconies.*
>
> *The Convention Center, built in 1888. At one time, it had a bowling alley and an auditorium for shows. People also used to just sit out on its balconies and look around. Because people were easily entertained before TVs, computers, and phones.*
>
> *The Pagoda Gift Shop, which was a post office back in*

*1915. Why a post office would be made to look like a
pagoda was now a mystery lost in time.*

In theory, they should start at the Eerie Estate first since
Boeckling lived there and maybe Collymore I was mad that he
owned the park. However, it wasn't actually only used during the
regular park season. It was only used as a haunted mansion during
the Halloween season in September and October. As a result, it
wasn't on any map Sloane or Amelia had been able to find. Even
with the help of librarian Belinda Gomez.

"Let's start with the Coliseum," Sloane said to Amelia as she
returned, now wearing a long, ruffled, pale purple gown and wide-
brimmed hat covered with violets. "Belinda found a bunch of post
cards from around 1915, and most of those showed the Coliseum.
It would have been a building that a lot of people thought of if you
said 'Cedar Point' to them. The Convention Center and the Pagoda
Gift Shop are close to it, so we can check them next."

A plan agreed upon, they left the Breakers Hotel (and any
ghosts that may or may not still be checked into it) for the amusement park (and any ghosts that may or may not still be riding roller
coasters there). The grannies and the Seifes went with them.

"If the park is haunted," Amelia observed, "then maybe the
ghost of Covington Collymore the First is still hanging out there.
Maybe we just need to hold a séance and ask him."

"NO!" Sloane and Brighton shouted together.

They looked at each other in surprise.

For a moment, Sloane thought maybe she'd connected with
the younger kid.

Then he buried his face in his tablet.

Moment. Over.

"I thought you didn't believe in ghosts," Amelia huffed, snapping open her lacy parasol to block out the sunlight as they left the lobby.

"I don't," Sloane said. "And I want to keep it that way."

Once inside the park, fun exploded upon them. Like someone had just popped open party-in-a-can and poured it all over everything. Buildings painted every color of the rainbow lined either side of the causeway. Music poured from an old-fashioned carousel as it spun round and round. Roller coasters swooped and soared from every possible direction, filling the air with screams of delight. Overhead, the sun glared down at them with blistering heat. At least the lake breeze puffed cool air off the water, scented with the sugary smell of slushies and the warm, greasy scent of hot dogs.

Granny Kitty and Granny Pearl took Skye and Brighton to play in the water feature midway down the causeway. Watching them go, Sloane twisted the tip of her ponytail round and round her fingertip. Why did Brighton feel about her the way Sloane felt about broccoli: something that smelled vaguely funky and was to be grimly, silently endured when it couldn't be avoided.

"I don't want to be broccoli." Sloane accidentally said it aloud.

"I don't want to be broccoli, either," Amelia agreed easily as she fiddled with her lacy parasol. "Do we need to worry about becoming broccoli?"

"I might." Sloane sighed. "Amelia, do you think Aiden and Ashley are good older siblings?"

"Definitely not!" Amelia said passionately. Then she thought it over a minute. "I mean, they want to be. They're just trying to be the big brother and sister they wished they'd had. Instead of trying to figure out what kind of older siblings I need them to be."

"I don't think Brighton likes me very much," Sloane admitted.

"He doesn't know you! He'll like you when he gets to know you," Amelia assured her, still fighting with her parasol, which had semi-collapsed.

Sloane took the parasol from her friend and snapped it into place. She didn't say that Brighton didn't seem to want to get to know Sloane, let alone like her.

Because right now, getting Brighton to like her wasn't going to help them catch the attention of BuzzFeed or Apple TV. Let alone help them find where Collymore's time capsule could be buried.

If it wasn't paved over by blacktop or concrete.

Which . . . didn't look promising.

Between rides, buildings, and walkways, most of the peninsula had been built—and rebuilt and then rebuilt again. There *were* lots of gardens, grassy areas, and tall, old trees. So, it wasn't completely hopeless.

But still not promising.

They walked along the causeway to the Coliseum. Sloane looked wistfully at the rides but reminded herself that they were here to work. Still, she had fond memories of coming to Cedar Point with her mom and dad and riding the coasters together. It would be nice to feel the way she'd felt then again.

Amelia, however, was not a fan of *any* ride. Not even the little kiddie rides that just spun slowly around in circles. Her few experiences with Cedar Point involved puking and clinging to turnstiles while her parents and siblings told her to give the rides another try.

She easily focused on filming as much of the park as she could. Then, later in the evening, she'd put together the first of their videos on the case and post it to YouTube for their followers.

And show both Mackenzie and CeeCee that she and Sloane weren't a couple of losers.

As well as hopefully, finally, catching the attention of BuzzFeed or Apple TV.

The Coliseum was a colorful building with lots of balconies, towers, and bay windows. Sort of like if someone took a castle and pressed a hand against it until it had been squashed more or less flat against the ground. Then painted it primary colors and added an enormous Ferris wheel behind it. Through the open doorways, lights flashed and shrill sounds escaped from an arcade inside.

To the Coliseum's left sat the Pagoda Gift Shop, a fake East Asian-style building. Or, at least, it was the style of what someone *thought* a pagoda looked like back in 1915. Rather like blocks stacked on top of each other, with each block smaller than the one below. The roofs all sloped downward and then curved back up again into points at the corners.

Both buildings were squeezed close together with little space between them. Certainly not enough for Sloane and Amelia to dig around in.

To the right of the gift shop and the Coliseum, the ground had been bricked over. Then covered with those slow-spinning little kid rides that scared Amelia and bored Sloane.

If the time capsule was buried there, they'd never be able to get to it.

In front of the Pagoda Gift Shop and the Coliseum stretched a large flower garden, splitting the causeway in two.

Sloane surveyed it as Amelia filmed. She joked, "I bet if we told my grannies those flowers are prize-winning, they'd have this dug up in no time."

"That might not be a terrible idea," Amelia said seriously as she handed her phone to Sloane. "Film me twirling my parasol over by the Coliseum. I'll walk from it to the Pagoda Gift Shop next door, and . . . hey, what are they doing over there?"

She pointed to the other side of the Pagoda Gift Shop, where there was normally another area of little kid rides. Those were all gone, with a half-built roller coaster bristling upward. Right now, it was all steel beams and concrete molds scratching at the sky. Only one hill had actually been built, and even it hadn't been completed.

A large chain-link fence warned away park-goers. A canvas sign stretched across it, announcing, master of mayhem! coming next year!

Which seemed like a warning, too.

As Sloane and Amelia watched, a man in an orange vest and a hard hat pulled a lever. A single carriage jugged up the hill. It began to wobble halfway up, making Amelia's palms sweat. Her stomach twisted itself into a sickly knot as the carriage rocked harder.

And harder.

"TURN IT OFF!" yelled a man on the ground. He wore a hard-hat and vest, too, and waved his arms about wildly.

The other man jerked the lever backward.

The car stopped shaking and glided back to its starting point.

Several people on the ground had a very angry conversation.

One that involved a lot of pointing, jabbing at the air, and jamming fists onto hips.

"Guess the Master of Mayhem is a new roller coaster," Sloane observed. "Not sure that I want to ride it. Right now, it seems like more of a Master of Mutilation."

"I *definitely* don't want to ride it." Amelia pressed a hand against her stomach. "But that's not what I'm talking about. What's up with the people digging in the dirt in front of the new roller coaster?"

Orange plastic fencing and yellow tape surrounded an area just to the side of the chain-link fence separating the construction site. Wood stakes poked up out of the dirt, with string running between them to form a grid. Flags had been stuck in some spots, while a bunch of teenagers and young adults bent over other spots. They all held trowels or brushes or the sort of sifters a kid might take to the beach. A tent without sides had been raised up on poles to provide a bit of shade.

A very pale, very bossy-looking boy of about eighteen or nineteen marched over to Sloane and Amelia. He carried a clipboard, wore a baseball cap, and had a sort of wound-up tightness about him. Like, at any moment, someone might press a lever and he'd shoot straight up into the sky and disappear somewhere over Lake Erie. "Hey! Stop leaning on that fence! You'll knock it over!"

"Oops. Sorry about that." Sloane straightened up and nudged Amelia to do the same. "What's going on here?"

The uptight teenager with the clipboard rolled his eyes at Sloane, "An archaeological dig, *obviously*. Now, go away before I call security and have you removed!"

"Jeez! Sorry!" Annoyed, Amelia scowled.

Not wanting to risk catching the attention of security, Sloane dragged her friend over to the shade of a nearby tree. Clipboard Boy watched them with arms crossed until he was sure they were leaving. After he returned to the hole beneath the tent, Sloane said, "An archaeological dig, huh? If Covington Collymore the First buried his time capsule there, then the archaeologists will find it before us! It'll ruin our investigation *and* our YouTube series."

Grimly, Sloane added, "And what do you want to bet that whoever runs Cedar Point gets to look at anything the archaeologists find? If there *is* a land deed inside that proves the first Collymore got swindled out of his land, they could easily make it disappear."

From the shade of the tree, they both turned their attention to the sweaty, dirty work going on over at the dig. Twirling her parasol thoughtfully, Amelia said, "Sloane, do you think it's possible that the people who run Cedar Point know about the time capsule? Do you think they could know that Covington Collymore is looking for it? And that they're trying to find it first?"

"I don't see how." Absently, Sloane reached up to find her long ponytail. She spun the tip of it around her fingertip. "Still, I wish we could get a better look at what they're doing."

Amelia brightened. "Oh, I have an idea!"

She marched over to a gap in the orange fencing, lifted up the caution tape . . .

. . . and simply stepped inside.

It didn't seem like much of an idea to Sloane. Who rushed over to join her friend.

Bossy Clipboard Boy raced over to Amelia, too.

"Didn't you hear me?" he huffed, reaching for a walkie-talkie clipped to his belt. "You need to get out of here right now!"

However, no matter how bossy or officious Clipboard Boy tried to be, he would never match the bossy officiousness of Amelia's family.

His words barely bounced off her. She gave another dismissive wave of her hand and kept right on walking. While Sloane remained nervously by the fencing.

Amelia lifted her nose into the air snootily. "I'm with the historical reenactors, *obviously*. I'm here to collect my research." When the boy looked at her blankly, Amelia raised an eyebrow. In her best Mac-Attack-Snyder imitation, she sneered, "You *do* have my research ready, right? If you don't have mine, what are you going to do when all the other reenactors show up?"

Sloane looked from the boy to Amelia and then back again, holding her breath. Could this actually work?

Clipboard Boy had taken the walkie-talkie off his belt. However, instead of using it, he said suspiciously, "I don't know what you're talking about."

"Look at my dress." With one gloved hand, Amelia lifted up her ruffled skirt. "Would I wander around dressed like someone out of the Victorian era if I wasn't a historical reenactor?"

"No one told me anything about this." Clipboard Boy scowled and an idea seemed to occur to him. "Hey, did Dr. Pickerington send you?"

"Er . . ." Amelia looked uncertainly at Sloane. Who shrugged helplessly in return. Clearly, there was a right or wrong answer to this question, but neither girl was certain what it was. Was it a good or bad thing to be sent by Dr. Pickerington?

"No," Sloane said right as Amelia said, "Yes."

He looked from one to the other of them in confusion. Behind him, the group of dust-covered teenagers stopped working to listen.

"Uh, I'm not," Sloane quickly explained, pointing first at herself and then at Amelia. "But she is."

He grimaced, more confused than ever.

But he put the walkie-talkie back on his belt.

"I need to ask Dr. Jamil about his," he said. "You'd better come with me. Though, if you're reenacting the park's Victorian period, I don't know why Dr. Pickerington would send you this way for anything other than a joke. We're looking for objects from the 1910s and '20s. Not from the Victorian era. Anyhow, follow me. Just be careful where you step, okay?"

With his clipboard, he gestured toward a building on the other side of the dig. He led the way toward it, with Sloane and Amelia following afterward.

To Amelia, Sloane whispered, "I can't believe that worked!"

Amelia shrugged. "Please, most of the time, my family has no idea what they're talking about. They just say it with a lot of confidence."

As they approached, the group of older teenagers stood up, clearly happy to have a reason to take a break. There were two boys and a girl. In spite of the raised canvas tent, all three of them were soaked in sweat and smeared with dirt.

A girl with pink-highlighted hair said, "Hey, look, guys. Ryan finally caught our ghost!"

She was clearly talking about Amelia, and everyone laughed. However, it wasn't a mean, laughing-at-you sort of laugh. Just a cheerful, hot-and-tired laugh.

Bossy Clipboard Boy Ryan, however, crossed his arms in annoyance. He hissed, "That isn't funny, Clara! Not with everything that's been going on!"

Sloane and Amelia exchanged surprised looks.

What was going on?

And did it have anything to do with Covington Collymore's missing time capsule?

Five

Ghosts are not the sorts of things most people worry about on a bright summer day when they're outside at an amusement park. There's something about the smells of freshly spun cotton candy and hot, buttered popcorn that are very antighost. If someone *was* to think about ghosts at Cedar Point, it wouldn't seem like such a bad thing to be haunted by one. What was it going to do? Lob candy apples at people? Taunt them with corn dogs? Force them to play the ring-toss game for all eternity?

(Actually, that one could be bad if the ghost didn't allow people to win. Ring-toss games are only fun when you have a chance of winning the giant stuffed animals watching you from the sides of the booth.)

However, when Ryan mentioned that the other teenagers shouldn't joke about ghosts, he looked around nervously. He even raised his clipboard to protect his face. Like he expected a ghost to spring up out of the ground and lob a water balloon at him or something.

"What's that about ghosts?" Sloane asked. While she didn't exactly believe in ghosts, she did worry about the possibility of clown ghosts.

If any place was likely to have clown ghosts, it was definitely going to be a one-hundred-and-fifty-year-old amusement park.

"Is it Maniac McGee?" Amelia asked eagerly, clutching her parasol. "Does the ghost look drowned? Oh! Or is it an elderly man, digging a hole and complaining about how this is his land?"

Sloane jammed an elbow into her friend's ribs, warning Amelia that she was saying too much.

Clara—the girl with the pink-highlighted hair—blinked in surprise. She wiped her forehead with the back of one gloved hand, leaving behind a trail of dirt. "Um, well, we haven't actually seen a ghost. So, we don't know if its Maniac McGee or some other ghost. But we've seen the damage he—or she!—has left behind."

"Clara!" Ryan warned, squeezing his clipboard the way a younger kid might clutch a teddy bear. "It's not professional to talk about ghosts! This isn't what an archaeological dig is supposed to be like! I wanted to be doing a dig over in Turkey or Greece or someplace respectable! Not digging up old roller coasters and getting my equipment broken by ghosts and—and—and having historical reenactors walk all over everything!"

"We're sorry," Sloane and Amelia squeaked together.

However, it was too late. Ryan stormed off.

"Don't worry about him." Clara grinned at them. She set down the trowel she'd been using and picked up a water bottle instead. "Ryan's always upset about something. This will save him the trouble of figuring out something else."

The two other teenagers both laughed. One boy was short, had dark brown skin, and wore glasses. The other was much taller, was a lighter brown, and still had braces on his teeth.

"I'm AJ." The boy with glasses smiled. "And this is Trent. Are you guys really historical reenactors? I mean, no offense, but *you* look like any kid, and *you* are not wearing a historically accurate outfit for the Victorian period." He pointed first at Sloane and then at Amelia.

"I'm not *not* a historical reenactor," Amelia said carefully. "We're filming a YouTube series, and I'm wearing this for certain scenes when we show the past. So, it doesn't have to be accurate. It just has to inspire the imagination."

All that was true.

Just none of it was being done with Cedar Point's actual permission.

Deciding they'd better get what information they could before they got thrown out of the dig, Sloane stepped in. "Ryan said you guys are looking for stuff from the 1910s and '20s. Have you found anything interesting so far?"

Like possibly a metal box or a wooden chest or anything else that Covington Collymore I might have buried?

(Not that Sloane said that.)

Trent nodded his head enthusiastically and flashed them his braces. "Definitely! We think some of the carnival games might have been over here. So far, we've found some scraps of striped fabric. Plus some BBs from the BB guns they used to shoot at the targets with. Um, some pennies, a rubber duckie—"

"And that creepy Kewpie doll," AJ cut in, shivering as he wiped a bit of mud from his glasses.

Clara grimaced as she swallowed a mouthful of water. "Okay, I'm not superstitious, but I'm telling you, digging up that thing is what caused the dig to become haunted."

"What's a Kewpie doll?" Amelia asked, hair already standing on end. She clutched her parasol more tightly. If Sloane had a horror of clowns, Amelia had a particular fear of dolls.

Clara took out her phone and pulled up a picture of one.

Sloane instantly developed a fear of Kewpie dolls, too.

Though it was more of a statue than an actual doll, it had big eyes, a very pointed head, and a sly smile.

The sly smile of a doll that was totally thinking about crawling all over you in your sleep.

"Eek!" Amelia backed away from the phone.

"I know, right?" Trent grabbed his water bottle. "Ever since we found that thing, all sorts of weird stuff has happened."

"Like . . . dolls trying to murder you?" Amelia asked faintly, looking this way and that. As though she thought the Kewpie doll might be wobbling toward her as they spoke.

Clara sat down on the edge of the hole to rest. "No, like our trowels and brushes breaking in the night. The sieves disappearing."

"And the only thing that showed up on the security camera video is a big orb of light," AJ chimed in. "Clara isn't the only one who thinks it's a ghost. Trent here thinks it's the ghost of Maniac McGee."

Trent almost choked on his water. "Do not! *You're* the one who brought up that guy. Though, if I had drowned after escaping from prison, I'd be mad too."

"That's no reason to take it out on our dig!" Clara objected indignantly. "If Murdock Maniac McGee decided to escape north across Lake Erie to Canada rather than heading south over land, that's not our fault."

Before Sloane and Amelia could find out more, Rigid Ryan returned, clipboard in hand and an extremely satisfied grin smeared across his face.

He'd brought along someone else.

"This is Dr. Jamil, and *he* says he hasn't heard anything about any historical reenactors!" Ryan crowed.

Dr. Jamil had salt-and-pepper hair and warm brown skin. He was probably about the age of Amelia's father, the Judge. Like the Judge, he had an air of authority that warned Amelia she'd better not try to hustle him. He looked more like a proper archaeologist than the teenage college students who worked for him. Even though he wore khaki shorts and a T-shirt and had slightly graying hair, there was something about Dr. Jamil that hinted he owned a leather jacket and fedora.

Like, at any moment in time, he might be called on to rescue some priceless artifact from history.

Suspecting that they might need help, Sloane discreetly sent her grannies a one-word message:

Help!

Since their phones were set up to track hers, Sloane hoped they'd figure out the rest.

"Should I call security?" Ryan asked, practically jumping up and down like a puppy about to get a treat. "No, wait! The police! No, wait! The FBI! No, wait! Homeland Security!"

Holding up a hand to calm down the over-eager college kid, Dr. Jamil said, "I'm sure none of that will be necessary."

"But, sir! They could be the ones breaking our equipment!

And deleting the files from our laptops!" As Ryan said this, Dr. Jamil cocked an exasperated eyebrow in his direction. Seeming to realize he'd said too much, Ryan buried his face in his clipboard.

Sitting over on the side of the dig hole, Clara, AJ, and Trent all snickered.

"Your laptop files have been deleted too?" Sloane flipped her ponytail over her shoulder in an effort to seem casual. "It's just that we heard that you were having some trouble here."

As Dr. Jamil turned to his four workers in exasperation, all of them suddenly became very interested in returning to work.

Shaking his head, Dr. Jamil said, "Just photographs of some very old maps of the peninsula. It isn't a really big deal, but they would have helped us avoid some of the buildings that were here before the Coliseum. Buildings that date before the 1920s and 1930s. The maps we were given by the park manager showed nothing here before 1905, but I would swear I saw a map somewhere that showed an old cabinetmaking shop and some other buildings from the 1860s or '70s."

"So, not having the maps makes it harder for you to know where to dig," Sloane summarized.

"It does." Dr. Jamil nodded. "We might accidentally destroy the remains of those buildings if we go about the dig in the wrong way."

"You might also 'accidentally' dig up things you're not supposed to," Amelia added.

Sloane and Amelia exchanged a look.

Covington Collymore VI had said that Covington Collymore

I made his fortune by building cabinets out of cedar trees. It had seemed like a weird way to become wealthy, but that was people in long-ago times for you.

Sometimes, they did weird things.

Like steal someone's cabinetmaking workshop and build an amusement park on top of it.

If Collymore's workshop had been here, then the land Zistel stole was *right here.*

Which also meant that Sloane and Amelia were right to suspect that the time capsule with the deed must be someplace close by.

Buried there during the time the professor and his students were looking for artifacts: the 1910s and 1920s.

Was it coincidence that the amusement park's manager had allowed an archaeological dig to search here?

Or were they looking for the deed too?

"I'm not sure what we would dig up that we're not supposed to." Dr. Jamil frowned and looked from one girl to the other. "Hey, what *are* you kids doing in here? Why *did* Dr. Pickerington send you? Is this some sort of joke? I didn't think she had a sense of humor."

Amelia gulped, while Sloane nervously played with her ponytail. Where were the grannies? Dr. Jamil seemed like someone who had heard a lot of excuses and nonsense from his students and was therefore pretty good at detecting a lie.

"Maybe we should walk over to the security station," he said slowly.

Luckily for the two of them, the grannies finally arrived.

"Oh good! You caught my parasol!" Granny Kitty cried,

wobbling under the yellow do not cross tape. Granny Pearl followed behind her, while Skye and Brighton remained next to the wagon pulling Bertram Cordelia. Skye crunched on a handful of Flavor-Blasted Goldfish crackers. While Brighton took one look at what was going on and buried his nose in his tablet.

For once, Sloane couldn't blame him for ignoring what was going on. Keeping his fingerprints off this train wreck seemed like a very good idea.

Both grannies moved as though extremely frail.

"What a good girl you are, Amelia," Granny Pearl said in a soft, quivery voice. "Helping out a tired old lady."

Granny Kitty took the parasol from Amelia and hefted it up onto her shoulder. She was bent over as though the weight of it was almost too much for her. To Dr. Jamil, she croaked, "The wind caught my umbrella and carried it away. My granddaughter and her little friend were kind enough to run after it for me."

"Hmmm . . ." Dr. Jamil narrowed his eyes and crossed his arms skeptically.

Ryan dropped his clipboard from his face and demanded, "Then why didn't you tell me that when I first caught you?"

That, Amelia could answer honestly. "Because I didn't want to get in trouble."

"Wait." Ryan frowned. "Weren't you carrying your parasol when you walked over here?"

He turned to Clara, Trent, and AJ for support.

"Nope," Clara said.

"Uh-uh," Trent agreed.

"Didn't see it," AJ confirmed.

"Uh-huh." Dr. Jamil clearly didn't buy it for a second. Still, he graciously offered an arm to either granny to lean on. He gallantly led them back to the yellow caution tape, with Sloane and Amelia following behind. "Should any of you lose any more items in the dig, please go to security. They will call me, and I'll be more than happy to retrieve them for you."

"Oh, thank you," Granny Pearl whispered. "You're *such* a gentleman."

"Yes," Dr. Jamil agreed. "I am. And as a gentleman, I won't point out that I saw the two of you easily pulling along that wagon. And lifting that concrete goose."

Granny Pearl forced out a smile. "So glad you're a gentleman, then."

"*So* glad," Granny Kitty agreed sweetly.

He nodded at them both and returned to his dig. Where Clara, AJ, and Trent were working once more, while ignoring Ryan's attempts to boss them around.

"Sloane-y." Granny Kitty put her hands on her hips and sourly watched him go. "Best avoid that one, if you can. He's too clever."

Sloane and Amelia couldn't help but agree.

They also very much wanted to know who erased the archaeologist's maps.

And was it to make sure that he dug in the wrong location?

Or perhaps it was better to say the *right* location.

The location where Covington Collymore I buried his time capsule.

Six

MAC ATTACK

Archaeologists aren't people to be trifled with. Anyone who has ever watched a movie or TV show knows that. The average archaeologist is armed with sharp picks and ropes. They have a tendency to be attacked by all sorts of evil people, monsters, and ghosts. (That might explain why Ryan was so nervous and aggressive.)

Archaeologists say that none of this actually happens in real life.

If you're an archaeologist who has been successfully attacked by evil people, monsters, or ghosts, you don't run around bragging about it.

Possibly, you can't.

Because you've been locked away deep in the bowels of the Sphinx by those evil people, monsters, or ghosts.

Regardless, Sloane and Amelia figured that Granny Kitty had a point about Dr. Jamil.

They all regrouped in the shade across the causeway from both the archaeological dig and the construction site for the new roller coaster, Master of Mayhem. (Or the Master of Mutilation, which was what Sloane was still calling it in her mind.)

"Hey, Brighton and Skye! Do you want a slushie?" Sloane asked in her best big-sister voice. "I'll buy you guys some!"

Skye scurried over, but Brighton remained by the flower garden running down the main causeway. He pulled out his tablet. "Thanks, but I don't want any."

Sloane cast about desperately in her mind. She remembered what Amelia had said earlier about how Aiden and Ashley always tried to be the big brother and sister they wished they could have had. Instead of the older siblings Amelia needed them to be. Sloane liked slushies, but Brighton liked . . . Brighton liked . . .

"Um, Poké Balls!" she cried, causing people around her to look at her weird. "There are Poké Balls over here!"

Several adults and kids rushed toward the slushie stand, phones and tablets in hand.

But not Brighton. He turned toward the spinning, flashing, stripe-tented rides on the other side of the causeway. "No thanks."

As Sloane yanked at her ponytail in frustration, Skye snatched the souvenir cup handed to her by a slushie stand worker.

"Thanks, Amelia!" she cried and skipped off to join her brother.

Glumly, Sloane watched the Seife kids leave with the grannies to return to the rides.

"Why couldn't Cynthia have had a pair of Labradoodles?" she asked Amelia. "I'm good with dogs."

Amelia made a sympathetic face. "They don't know how lucky they are. Brighton and Skye should try spending a day with Aiden and Ashley. Here, have a slushie."

She handed Sloane an enormous, rainbow-hued slushie in a souvenir cup. As they settled onto a bench, the Master of Mayhem builders sent another car up the hill.

This time it made it an even shorter distance before it started to rock violently.

Immediately, the ride operator brought it back down again.

More angry shouting filled the air from the designers and the builders. Even over the roar of the working, already-built roller coasters and their screaming riders.

"I think someone made a mistake in their design," Sloane observed.

"Yeah, and that mistake was to design something called the Master of Mayhem in the first place." Amelia shuddered. Then, sucking on her curvy straw, she said, "Who do you think Dr. Pickerington is?"

"I'm not sure." Sloane poked at the red, orange, and yellow layers of her drink to blend the flavors together. "But I got the sense that Dr. Jamil doesn't like her. What I want to know is, why is there an archaeological dig at an amusement park?"

"An archaeological dig poking around right where Covington Collymore the First probably buried his time capsule with the deed." Releasing her straw, Amelia poked her finger up into the air. In an English accent, she said, "Coincidence, I think not!"

(She meant to sound like Sherlock Holmes, but actually sounded more like Bert the chimney sweep from *Mary Poppins*.)

Sloane scooped up some of the flavored ice in her cup. "It's definitely not a coincidence that their tools keep getting broken."

Sloane pulled up the park map on the Cedar Point app she'd installed on her phone. She zoomed in on the area of the dig.

"For sure, they're digging pretty close to all the buildings we're interested in. See, the Convention Center is on the north side of it, while the Coliseum and the Pagoda Gift Shop are on the south side. We still don't know where the Eerie Estate is, and the Breakers Hotel is another place where it could be buried. But that's three of the five buildings where it could be. So, yeah, it seems like too much of a coincidence that the time capsule might be there and archaeologists are digging there *and* someone is breaking their tools."

"Unless it's either Dr. Pickerington or Maniac McGee playing a prank." Amelia pressed the frosty side of her souvenir cup against her face to cool it down. Her phone vibrated and she picked it up. "Ugh. It's my mom."

Quickly, she placed it face down on the picnic table. Then she hid behind her giant cup like she thought her mom might actually crawl through the screen to see what Amelia was doing.

"We're all in family therapy now, you know," Amelia told Sloane when the phone finally stopped ringing. Until it did, Sloane had busied herself with swirling together the green, blue, and purple layers of her slushie. "You know, so we can understand each other better? And, like, figure out how to talk to each other without judging?"

"How's that going?" Sloane thought she had a pretty good idea of the answer.

Amelia shrugged and came out from behind her cup. "I don't know. Okay I think? After the first session, our therapist looked like she'd been hit by a tornado and suggested that we all see our own, individual therapists *plus* see her as a family. Like, I think she knew she couldn't handle all of us on her own. So she's pretty smart."

"No offense, but I think it's pretty obvious that your family is *a lot*." Sloane grinned at her friend.

Amelia snorted. "I'm not offended. I say that all the time. At least Cynthia Seife's kids seem nice. Even if they aren't Labradoodles. Skye's especially cute."

As if sensing that she was being talked about, Skye waved at them from the ride she was on.

Somewhere, somehow—probably in one of the gift stores—she'd gotten a pair of long gloves like Amelia's. Hers were purple instead of white, but it was still very clear who the little kid was trying to look like.

Amelia waved back at Skye. The little girl's worship seemed to give Amelia courage. Picking up her phone, she FaceTimed her mother back. It turned out that Amanda Miller was anxious because Amelia hadn't posted any videos to YouTube yet, and Amanda worried that meant something was wrong.

Amelia explained that she was still editing their first video before she could upload it. Her mom seemed relieved, and it was all fine. Still, sometimes, it felt to Amelia like her family didn't understand how much effort went into the investigations and videos that she and Sloane did. Sure, they were supportive of her work, and that was a *huge* improvement in how they used to treat her in their well-intentioned-but-incredibly-insensitive way, but . . .

It was still frustrating to have her family not understand that what Amelia was doing was actually pretty difficult.

To them, it seemed like she and Sloane had gained over fifty thousand subscribers just by wandering around, asking questions, and filming what they did.

When, in fact, they had to do a lot of research. Read a lot of boring things. And then wade through hours of video to find the good stuff.

Waving goodbye to her mom, Amelia ended the call and said, "Let's go over to the Convention Center. We can use the bathrooms and check out the other side of the building. Dr. Jamil might be digging in the wrong place because Covington Collymore the First *might* have buried his deed on the other side."

Going to the Convention Center, they found the bathroom doors on the outside of the building. They used them, and then Sloane filmed Amelia twirling her parasol and generally looking old-fashioned next to the building. Afterward, they checked out its north side, the side away from the archaeological dig.

Yup. It looked like a building.

Yup, it was old.

And if anything was buried on three of its sides, they'd need a jackhammer and a backhoe to make it through all the bricks, concrete, and blacktop.

If Covington Collymore I buried his deed there, they had absolutely no hope of finding it.

By now, the sun blazed ferociously in the sky, scaring away the breeze from Lake Erie. Without it, not even Amelia's parasol provided enough shade to keep both girls from panting with the heat. As sweat trickled grossly down their backs, they decided to cool off inside the Convention Center's air-conditioning.

They instantly regretted that decision.

Girls and boys in tight, sparkly costumes filled the lobby. They stood by long tables as their coaches signed them in. Anything in the room that could be covered in glitter and swag had been covered in glitter and swag. Gold-and-silver balloon bouquets framed a banner above the doors into a larger room. It read, WELCOME TO THE 21ST ANNUAL CEDAR POINT DANCE COMPETITION.

The dance competition! Where Mackenzie and CeeCee would be lurking, waiting to mock Osburn and Miller-Poe Investigations.

"Eek! Let's get out of here," Amelia squeaked. She whipped around and tried to run, but got caught up in the swirl of her long skirts. Her parasol went one way and Amelia went another.

The umbrella clubbed a coach on the head, knocking the woman flat onto the table where she'd been scribbling on a form. Amelia fell against two dancers in scarlet-and-blue athletic suits.

They staggered and caught her as the coach tried to right herself too, legs flailing frantically in the air.

The entire room went quiet, turning to see what was going on.

Feeling the heat rise in her face, Sloane scooped up the umbrella and snapped it shut. Then she grabbed Amelia from the two very annoyed dancers.

Together Sloane and Amelia helped pull the coach off the table and back onto her feet.

When they turned back around, they discovered that everyone was *still* staring at them.

Then a snicker cut through the air.

Mackenzie, CeeCee, and their entire dance team stood in the doorway, backlit by the sunlight beyond.

Watching everything.

With a smirk, Mackenzie nodded at her teammates. "Remember what we practiced?"

Immediately, they broke into dance moves.

Dance moves that spelled out letters.

L-O-S-E-R-S.

While Grandma Snyder filmed it all and couldn't look prouder.

The woman Amelia had pulled off the table crossed her arms in annoyance. "Girls, it is not good sportsmanship to say something like that about the other teams!"

Smiling fiendishly and looking right at Sloane and Amelia, Mackenzie said, "We weren't referring to the other teams."

"Oh." The coach followed Mackenzie's gaze. Only then did Sloane and Amelia notice that she was wearing a silver-and-black athletic suit almost identical to those worn by Mackenzie's dance team. In a less convincing voice, she said, "That's not very nice, either . . . I suppose."

"Oh dear!" Grandma Snyder clucked. "Already uploaded it to TikTok!"

Sloane and Amelia took one look at each other and silently agreed to get the heck out of there.

Unfortunately, Mackenzie's dance team still blocked the exit. So, the two of them turned around and ran the other way. Feeling very like the room was full of dancer zombies who might devour them with laughter and embarrassing TikTok videos at any moment.

They finally ended up in a rather boring hallway with plain walls, plain doors, and sturdy carpeting. The lights overhead seemed to have been designed for HalloWeekends. (That is, Halloween Weekends squashed together into one word. Like it was so scary that the words themselves had to press together to stay safe from anything that might jump out at them.) Because it made both Sloane and Amelia look sickly and half dead.

"Ugh. We are *not* filming anything here." Amelia grimaced as she checked out her face in her camera. "I look like the ghost of Maniac McGee."

"I think these must be offices," Sloane observed. She looked at the time on her phone. "Hm. It's lunchtime, and no one seems to be around."

Amelia considered the long row of doorways. "I suppose it would be wrong to break into any of them and look for clues. You know, about why Dr. Jamil is digging right where the time capsule might be buried. Or who Dr. Pickerington is. Or whether or not Maniac McGee is a real ghost who doesn't like archaeologists. It would be wrong to break in and find the answers to those things."

"Break in, yes." Sloane walked down the hallway. "But . . . if anyone left any doors open, we could go in. You know, just to ask for help getting out of the building."

There was a red exit sign directly above her head as she said this.

However, Amelia decided to go along with the story and not point this out. As she followed Sloane through an open door, she said, "You know, you sound a little bit like your grannies."

"I think they might be a bad influence," Sloane admitted.

The first two open doors led them into offices that didn't have anything particularly useful inside. One person was a big Ohio State Football fan and had filled the room with helmets, bobble-heads, posters, and other souvenirs. The next office appeared to be a shrine to the same three kids given that every wall and surface was covered with their photographs.

"Either those are someone's kids. Or else they committed one heck of a crime," Sloane said.

Neither Sloane nor Amelia felt comfortable going through either person's computer or desk drawers. The grannies probably would have, but they didn't.

They went into the last open doorway. It led into a room bigger and more elegant than the other two. Like someone had been paid to decorate it in a sleekly modern style. It reminded Amelia uncomfortably of her family's home, actually.

Even if her family's home didn't have a bunch of blueprints and old, yellowed maps pinned to the wall.

Or a model of a roller coaster inside a huge clear glass box, sitting on a table in the middle of the room.

"Hey, whoa! I bet this is what the Master of Mutilation—I mean, the Master of Mayhem—is going to look like when it's done." Distracted from their search for clues, Sloane went over to look at it. "Wow! Amelia, check this out! This actually looks like a lot of fun. You know, if they can get the cars to stop falling off that first hill. It's sort of like the Valravn, but with more twists, and you go upside down a lot more. And . . . Amelia, are you going to throw up? What's wrong?"

Leaning on her parasol for support, Amelia managed not to vomit. She'd gone quite green in the face as she looked at the model and listened to Sloane describe the ride. Taking off her long gloves, she used them to fan her skin.

"I don't like roller coasters," she managed to say through clenched teeth, still battling with a terrified stomach.

"But we aren't going to ride it. We're just looking at it."

"Yeah, well, I *really* don't like roller coasters."

"Good," a woman's voice behind them said. "Because you have no right to be looking at this one."

Before either Sloane or Amelia could turn around, a hand gripped each of them by the shoulder.

Security!

They'd forgotten the most important step in committing a crime.

Don't get caught.

Seven

Getting caught is something you should avoid if you're committing a crime like breaking-and-entering. Actually, you should just avoid committing crimes, if you possibly can. That's always good life advice.

However, when you're a detective like Sloane and Amelia are, sometimes you had to do things that were the teensy-weensy-itty-bittiest bit—er—*illegal*. Like breaking-and-entering. (Which is what someone does when they go someplace they aren't supposed to go—like someone's office—to look at stuff that is none of their business—like models for new roller coasters.)

So, yes, when doing all that, it's best not to get caught.

Or you might do what Amelia did when she got caught.

Which was to run over to a trash can and urp slushie into it.

Sloane was left behind on her own to deal with the annoyed-looking woman who had caught them. Rather than a security guard uniform, she wore sensible heels and a plum-colored pantsuit that looked amazing with her dark skin. She tapped a foot irritably against the carpeted floor.

"Er, Dr. Pickerington?" Sloane guessed.

She'd actually seen the woman before—over at the construction site for the new roller coaster. This woman had been watching as the workers tried out a car on the first hill.

The question about Dr. Pickerington caught the woman off guard. Well, maybe it wasn't Sloane's question. Maybe it was Amelia bent over the trash can. Either way, the woman shook her head. "No, I'm Jayla Rychner, and I'm the operations manager for this park. What are the two of you doing in my office?"

Slayer Sloane remembered the excuse she'd come up with earlier. "We were trying to find the exit, and we got lost."

"Hm. You look old enough to follow the exit signs." Jayla Rychner stepped between Sloane and the roller-coaster model, blocking her view of it.

Over by the garbage can, Amelia straightened up. She was closer to the blueprints and old, yellowing maps than either Sloane or the park manager. Unsurprisingly, the blueprints seemed to be of the Master of Mayhem.

More surprisingly, the maps showed buildings from around the time Zistel built his first bathing house and swindled Covington Collymore I out of his land.

Were these the maps that had been stolen from the archaeology dig?

If so, had Jayla Rychner stolen them?

And why? Couldn't she have just asked Dr. Jamil for them?

Amelia pulled out her phone and quickly took a few pictures before Jayla Rychner remembered that there was a second intruder in the room. As the park manager turned toward her, Amelia shoved her phone into her pocket.

"What are you doing over there? Those documents are private!" Jayla Rychner marched over past Amelia and pushed a button on the wall. A velvet curtain glided across the maps and blueprints, hiding them.

Amelia panicked. She theatrically stretched out a hand for Jayla Rychner to shake. "Oy do de-clah! How trilled oy am to meet ya!"

Jayla. Rychner blinked several times very quickly. "I have no idea what you're doing, but please stop it."

She sounded like Amelia's mother. Combined with her suit, she reminded Amelia a little too much of Amanda Miller.

"Trying to be British," Amelia admitted in a small voice, shoulders slumping. "I thought you'd be less mad if we were British."

The park manager looked from Amelia to Sloane—and then back to Amelia again. Then she closed her eyes, put a hand to her forehead, and sighed deeply. When she opened her eyes again, she said, "Why don't you follow me, and I'll get you back to the dance competition so you can find your parents. Thank goodness a very helpful dancer let me know that a couple of kids had wandered down this way!"

With that, she pushed them both out of her office, closing the door, and leading them down the hall. As they went, Sloane whispered to Amelia, "How much do you want to bet that Mackenzie was that 'helpful dancer'? Why can't she leave us alone?"

Heat flared through Amelia's whole body. What if Mackenzie had cost them the chance to find clues in Jayla Rychner's office? Clues that would have solved this case—and even that BuzzFeed or Apple TV deal?

Outrage at Mackenzie gave Amelia enough nerve to ask Jayla Rychner a question. "Hey, are those the same maps that were stolen from Dr. Jamil's archaeological dig?"

Jayla Rychner froze.

"What do you know about that?" she demanded. "*How* do you know anything about that?"

Sloane cut in, saying innocently, "Oh! Er, we just heard him talking with one of his students when we were over by the dig. Why is there an archaeological dig at the park, anyhow? It just seems kind of strange."

They had almost reached the lobby area. Jayla Rychner stopped and gnawed her lip, like she was thinking about just shoving Sloane and Amelia in that direction without answering Sloane's question. Then, slowly, she said, "Ohio law requires businesses to have archaeologists come in and excavate land that has 'historical value' before anything can be built on it. Since Cedar Point has been around for a hundred-and-fifty years, pretty much everything is of historical value. So, when we decided to tear down some old rides and build a new one, we had to let them do a dig anyplace that hadn't been checked in the past. Most of the land for our new coaster had already been excavated before. However, the part nearest the Coliseum and gift shop haven't, so we've had to make a few changes to construction. Which is fine! It hasn't caused any problems at all!"

The park manager said it too forcefully, gritting the words out between her teeth as she tried to stretch a smile across her face.

Unfortunately, it ended up as more of a grimace.

A grimace that said everything wasn't fine.

Said it as loudly as a roller-coaster car crashing to the ground, if it fell off its tracks.

Collecting herself, Jayla Rychner returned to the question about the maps. "Anyhow, Dr. Jamil doesn't need those maps. They're nothing to do with his dig."

With that, she left them to return to her worries about the crashing coaster. Sloane and Amelia hurried across the lobby and out the double doors before Mackenzie or CeeCee could spot them. As soon as they left the air-conditioning, the thick heat and humidity of the summer day wrapped around them like soggy blankets. Amelia pulled out her phone and swiped up the pictures she'd taken of the maps.

"Sloane, she's lying!" Amelia cried excitedly. "These maps show buildings from back in the 1860s and 1870s. They have to be copies of the ones that were stolen—and Dr. Jamil said he needed those."

"But why would she do that?" Grabbing the phone from Amelia, Sloane used her fingers to zoom in. "Does it show any of the land as belonging to Covington Collymore the First?"

"I don't think so." Amelia peered over her friend's shoulder. "But I think it does say what some of the buildings were."

Going over to a shady spot under some trees, they moved the map round and round, zooming in and out. The ink was very old and wavery, browned with time. It marked the bathhouses close to the lake, along with a beer garden, whatever that was. Several cedar groves were also drawn, along with an outhouse factory and a coffin factory.

"What are outhouses again?" Amelia asked, positive she should know but unable to remember all the same.

Sloane snickered. "They're little houses with toilets inside. Well, not toilets. Wooden benches that you sat on that had a hole cut in them so you could—you know—do your business. Like, into an actual hole because this was before plumbing. My grannies say our house had one because it was built in 1880. Granny Kitty says that it was probably back by the alleyway and that's why the flower gardens do so well out there."

Amelia wasn't at all sure how using part of a backyard as a toilet could help flowers grow.

And she didn't want to know either.

Moving on quickly from that, she said, "That seems like a weird thing to build right next door to a place that's made coffins. And bad news for Covington Collymore the Sixth. Because I don't see a cabinetmaking workshop, and that's how the first Collymore made his money. If it was anywhere around, I'd think it would be on this map. Maybe he has the location totally wrong."

This was both an excellent and disappointing thought.

Maybe Covington Collymore I hadn't owned a cabinetmaking workshop here at all.

Maybe family legend had somehow twisted up all the facts.

Moved the workshop from one side of the peninsula to the other.

If the cabinetmaking workshop wasn't near Zistel's bathhouse and beer garden, then he'd have no reason to steal Collymore I's land. It wasn't like Zistel bought up the entire peninsula. That had happened slowly over a period of twenty or thirty years.

Could Sloane and Amelia be looking for something that had never existed?

This was a depressing thought, and one that required more carnival food in their stomachs than just slushies. They walked down the causeway, past more rides and roller coasters. Shrieking people spun and zipped past, hands in the air. Each time they did, Amelia flinched and gripped her umbrella more tightly.

She was *really* not a fan of amusement parks.

Well, the rides anyhow. She liked french fries in little paper trays just fine. Sloane got some for both of them while Amelia refilled their souvenir cups with more slushies. Then they settled down beneath a triangular sunshade to eat their fried food and to look over the map again.

"Bathhouses, beer garden, outhouse factory, and coffin shop," Sloane listed them again with a sigh.

"Ugh." Amelia made a frustrated face. She scowled at her phone. "We've got to be missing something. Otherwise, why would Jayla Rychner lie to Dr. Jamil about these buildings? Do you think it's the coffin factory? Too creepy, do you think? I mean, why would they even need coffins here? Unless there's a cemetery here and they're trying to hide it?"

"I don't think so. The whole amusement park turns into one big cemetery for HalloWeekends in September and October." Sloane made a face that matched Amelia's as she dunked a french fry in some ketchup. "As for the coffins, I don't know. Burial at sea? Or—I guess—burial on the Great Lakes? When we were at the library in Wauseon, Belinda mentioned that lots of ships have gone down in the storms on Lake Erie. And a lot of those sailors didn't survive. The ghost of Maniac McGee would have plenty of company in the water."

"Maybe that's why he haunts Cedar Point," Amelia joked. "Too crowded in the water!"

Sloane laughed at that, then stopped. A sudden image of a whole crowd of ghosts wading out of the lake filled her head. She shivered at the thought and pushed it quickly away. The trouble with being friends with Amelia was that her imagination was so good, it could sometime infect Sloane's, too.

"But they wouldn't need coffins for those guys," she said before Amelia could say anything more about ghosts. "Let's give Belinda Gomez a call and see if she has any idea why there would be a coffin shop here. Maybe it's a clue, somehow. That or the outhouse factory!"

They FaceTimed the librarian, catching her as she was closing up the Wauseon Public Library for the afternoon. She already sat on her motorcycle, a helmet on her head. Her German shepherd, Bunny, peered over her shoulder with a pair of goggles on his eyes.

Even through the speakers, the bike's engine roared loud enough that it startled a nearby toddler, causing him to drop his ice-cream cone.

"'Sup?" Belinda asked, lifting up her visor and cutting the engine. The shrieks of a very unhappy little boy replaced its mechanical thunder.

Sloane shoved her phone at Amelia and hurried over to the ice-cream stand to replace the kid's cone and apologize to his mom. She looked like she'd had enough of the amusement park to last her a lifetime. And might start sobbing right along with her kid. So Sloane bought her an ice-cream cone too.

Amelia explained what was going on as Bunny tried to lick her through the screen.

Belinda didn't need to look anything up to know the answer. "Coffins were made out of wood back then. Still are, sometimes. Usually, they were made out of pine, but cedar would have worked too."

"But Collymore was using the cedar grove for his cabinets. And there's this outhouse factory, too," Sloane pointed out as she sat back down again. "Would there be enough cedar trees around here for all that?"

Bunny slurped the screen. From behind a wavery veil of drool, Belinda explained, "It's possible that his cabinetmaking workshop and the coffin store were one and the same. Back then, lots of cabinetmakers also made coffins and buried people. Neither was enough to make a living, but together, you could get by on the money you made. After Covington Collymore the First became rich, it probably sounded more respectable to say he made his money in cabinets than to say he made it selling coffins."

"Wait, though." Now Amelia had an objection. She fanned her face, which had gone sweaty and blotchy. "You just said that people could barely make a living making furniture and coffins. Then how could he have gotten rich that way?"

"Dunno. Maybe by selling the land he owned to that Zistel guy." Belinda used her sleeve to wipe her screen. Bunny seemed to think that meant she wanted him to lick it again. "If I was you, I'd go to the Sandusky County Courthouse and see what you can find. Maybe Collymore hasn't found anything there because he doesn't *want* to find anything there."

She rang off as Bunny's tongue found the camera lens again.

Sloane and Amelia looked at each other without much enthusiasm.

If Belinda was right, Covington Collymore VI wasn't going to like what they'd found.

And neither would their YouTube subscribers.

Eight

AMELIA DISCOVERS A SECRET, UNWANTED TALENT

Disappointments are part of life, of course.

When you're a detective, disappointments are an even bigger part of life. If every clue turned up a lead and an "Ah-HA!" moment, everyone would be a detective. If finding a hidden treasure—or at the very least, a hidden land deed—could be done in half a day, no one would need Osburn and Miller-Poe Investigations.

Still, it was one thing for a mystery to be difficult to solve.

It was quite another for a mystery to not exist at all.

"Do you think this whole thing could just be a big misunder-standing?" Amelia asked unhappily, pushing aside her paper tray of fries. She was suddenly no longer hungry.

"Maybe. That makes a lot more sense than Collymore the First getting incredibly rich by selling coffins and cabinets." Even though she felt as down as Amelia, Sloane kept on scarfing her fries. "What a weird combination, by the way. Like, can you imag-ine selling those things? 'Hi! Would you like a cabinet to store your dishes in? Or would you prefer one for storing dead bodies? Our cabinets come in handy in all sorts of situations!'"

Amelia snickered and picked up another fry herself. She dunked it in ketchup but couldn't quite bring herself to eat it.

"Okay, let's say that Collymore sold his land to Zistel. Then what was he talking about in his letter?"

Sloane took out her phone and swiped up the picture she'd taken of it back at the Red Rambler Coffee House.

My Dearest Petunia,

The events of 1875 have always weighed heavily upon my mind. Reverend Callender says that the truth will set me free. But I fear that truth cannot be known before my death. Like a ship on Lake Erie, I can feel myself sailing off into my final sunset. I've hidden a box near the land from which I ran my business. When it's found, all will know what really happened. The corner stone on which all lies rest will show itself to be a fake and crumble. Until then—"The great ships sail outward and return, bending and bowing o'er the billowy swells."

Your devoted husband,

Covington

Having finished reading it, Sloane and Amelia looked at each other.

"He's definitely not happy about something," Amelia admitted. "And whatever it was, it happened in 1875. Which is when Zistel really started expanding his business. But . . . I don't know. That still doesn't prove that Zistel stole Collymore's land."

Leaving the letter open on her phone, Sloane reached over and picked up Amelia's. She found the photograph of the old map again. "It looks like the bathhouses, the outhouse factory, and Collymore's workshop all touched the water. And they're all more or less near the Coliseum, the Convention Center, and the Pagoda Gift Shop."

"Which puts us back pretty much where we started." Amelia sighed.

Sloane matched her sigh. "Guess we need to ask my grannies to take us to the courthouse."

"Yeah, I guess." Amelia couldn't make herself sound enthusiastic.

It wasn't that either one of them objected to going to the courthouse and poking through old records. Not exactly. As investigators of historical crimes and mysteries, they were used to pouring over boring books and documents.

It was just . . . well, courthouses tended to be old, dark, and gloomy—and filled with a musty smell. One so thick, it seemed to blanket all the rooms and be the cause of the dark and the gloom.

Whereas happy sunshine filled the air of Cedar Point.

Air that smelled like cotton candy.

It wasn't easy to be enthusiastic about exchanging sugar and fun for dust and quiet.

Sloane wiped the sweat from her brow with a napkin and tried to look at the bright side. "At least the courthouse should be air-conditioned!"

"Not necessarily," Amelia said. As the daughter of a judge, she had some experience with the courthouses around the state of Ohio. "Sometimes, only some of the rooms are air-conditioned. The rest are hot and stuffy."

"Just let me have this for now, okay?"

They trudged off to find Granny Kitty, Granny Pearl, and the two Seife kids. They found them in the bouncy house. Well, Skye and Brighton were in the bouncy house. The two grannies had conned a group of parents into a game of old maid.

For money.

"Sloane-y!" Granny Kitty cried, jumping when she saw her granddaughter. She elbowed Granny Pearl—who laid down her last pair of cards. Sticking a dad in a gingham shirt and cargo shorts with the old maid card. Granny Pearl swept a large mound of dollar bills into her fanny pack.

Sloane rubbed at her forehead with a finger and thumb. "Grannies, you promised you wouldn't do anything illegal!"

"Oh, we're just having a little fun! Aren't we?" Granny Kitty pinched the cheek of the man in the gingham shirt. Both he and the other dads seemed pretty sheepish about being hustled by a couple of ladies in their seventies. They gathered up their kids and strollers and hurried off to find their partners for protection.

"Who wants ice cream?" Granny Pearl waved around some of the dollars she'd just won.

Before either Sloane or Amelia could answer, Brighton spotted them through the bouncy house's safety netting. He made a face at Sloane like she was a recess monitor who had just blown the whistle to tell everyone it was time to go back inside the school building. What was *with* this kid? The only other person who had disliked Sloane this much was . . . well, Amelia. Back before they became friends.

. If Brighton wasn't exactly enthusiastic to see Sloane and Amelia, his sister had no such problems. Skye let out a squeal and rushed out to hug Amelia, with Brighton following sluggishly behind. Not used to people being this happy to see her, Amelia wasn't prepared for it. When Skye crashed into her, Amelia fell backward into a flower garden for the second time in a day.

Taking Skye with her.

Once more, petals flew everywhere.

When they struggled up out of the pink and yellow petunias, Skye grinned happily and clapped her hands together. "Yay! Let's do that again! But this time, I'm gonna throw Bertram Cordelia at you!"

"NO!" everyone shouted together before she could bludgeon Amelia to death with a concrete lawn ornament.

Skye seemed confused by why no one else thought this was a good idea. But she went along with it happily enough. "Amelia, go on the swings with me! You'll go on the swings with me, right? Brighton says they're for babies, but I'm not a baby, and *I* like them!"

Amelia hesitated for a moment. Her instinctive reaction was not just, *NO!* but a full on *NO WAY! UH-UH! I'M OUT OF HERE!*

But...

Skye was just asking about swings. Those should be fine.

Amelia didn't mind playground swings and slides and things like that.

By the time she realized that Skye meant the sort of swings that swung round and round at a high rate of speed, high up in the air, it was too late.

Skye had already tugged her into joining a line that was too short to allow Amelia to see the ride. When she did, her panicked brain froze.

The next thing Amelia knew, Skye was clapping happily.

As a bored ride attendant strapped them into their swings.

"No," Amelia whispered. But the word came out so small and dry that the wind caught it like a dried-out blade of grass. Whisking it away to die over the lake.

Having not heard her, the attendant moved on to the next kid.

"Uh, no." This time, Amelia said it more strongly. Skye turned and blinked at her questioningly.

"Do you have to go to the bathroom?" the little girl asked, concerned.

"Yes! Yes, that's it!" Amelia grasped this suggestion like a floaty tossed to a drowning person.

"Don't worry," Skye assured her. "If you pee your pants, it'll go out into the air and everyone will think it's just mist from the white water rapids ride."

"*What?*" That was it. Amelia struggled to free herself from her harness.

Unfortunately, it was too late. The teenager running the ride grasped the "start" lever with both hands and yanked it forward.

The ride shuddered.

Then began to twirl.

Slowly, at first. Giving Amelia hope that she might be able to slither over the straps before the swing rose too high in the air.

Then faster . . .

. . . and faster.

"STOP! I HAVE TO GO TO THE BATHROOM!" Shrieking, Amelia clutched one rope with both hands.

"*WHEEEEEE!*" Skye shrieked right along with her. "Isn't this fun, Amelia?"

Amelia, however, was past speech.

Up, up, up, the swings lifted her. Then, the centrifugal forces her seventh-grade science teacher, Mrs. Lemons, had taught her about pushed her swing outward. Farther and farther, until both the swing and Amelia were parallel to the ground.

Still spinning.

The world around Amelia blurred together, becoming nothing more than a green smudge of trees, dotted with the various other colors of people and their shirts.

All the junk food she'd eaten united together in her stomach and came to an agreement to escape. Amelia squeezed her jaw shut, determined to keep them trapped inside.

Round and round and round, they went.

Tighter and tighter, Amelia squeezed the rope.

Harder and harder, she clenched her jaw.

Until finally—*finally!*—the spinning slowed. The swings drooped. Amelia's feet found the concrete.

But she couldn't let go of the rope. No matter how hard she tried to release her fingers, they just wouldn't do it.

Skye came over to help. Then Brighton, followed by the grannies and Sloane.

"Hey, you have to get off the ride and get back in line, if you want to go again!" The ride operator put his fists on his hips in annoyance.

Go again??? *Go again!!!*

The horror of that thought was enough to shoot Amelia up and out of the swing's harness without actually releasing it.

She landed with a thud on the ground.

The force of which finally released the contents of her stomach for the second time in the day.

Amelia hurled all over the grannies nice, clean shoes and the legs of their floral track suits.

"Ewwww!" Everyone standing nearby in line retched and scurried away.

Skye and Brighton retreated to the safety of the wagon.

The grannies gaped in horror.

"I'm sorry." Amelia clapped her hands over her mouth, terrified that something else might try to escape. Her throat burned like it had been scalded with acid. Which, technically, it had been.

Sloane raced to the closest concession stand and returned with bottles of water. One for Amelia, and two more for the grannies to use to clean off their shoes and pants.

"I, uh, suppose now is a bad time to ask for a ride to the Sandusky County Courthouse, huh?" Sloane asked.

The looks both grannies gave her very clearly said, "Yes. Now is *not* a good time to ask."

"Wow. You even puke better than other people," Skye informed Amelia solemnly, eyes huge with awe. "How come you're so good at everything?"

Granny Kitty and Granny Pearl took Brighton, Skye, the wagon, and Bertram Cordelia back to the Breakers Hotel. The grannies both needed a shower and a change of clothes. While the two Seife kids wanted to rest in the air-conditioning for a little bit. Brighton seemed especially eager to get away, but for once, that seemed to be because of Amelia rather than Sloane.

In spite of Skye's praise, tears of embarrassment welled in

Amelia's eyes. She'd totally made a mess of everything! Sloane's grannies had been nice enough to bring them to Cedar Point, and in return, she had thrown up on them. Which was both gross and rude. Now, instead of helping Sloane and Amelia follow up on a lead, Granny Kitty and Granny Pearl had to take a break to clean up.

Leaving Sloane and Amelia behind without any other clues or ideas.

That was it. Amelia couldn't keep the tears back any longer.

They overflowed and ran down her cheeks.

Realizing people were watching them, Sloane grabbed her friend and dragged her away.

They didn't stop until they'd reached the Frontier Trail. This part of the park was shady, with lots of old-fashioned buildings like log cabins and wooden-framed store buildings. Sloane found a stone wall for the two of them to sit on so Amelia could finish off the rest of her water in peace.

"I mess everything up," Amelia snuffled into her bottle. "Mackenzie makes fun of me. I fall into things. I threw up *twice.*"

Sloane twisted her ponytail around her fingertip, her own stomach knotted up with contact anxiety. She knew exactly how Amelia felt. It didn't matter how good Sloane was at things like softball or volleyball. The minute she missed a ball or didn't reach a base in time, she felt like the absolute worst.

Which was how she was feeling right now about Brighton. Something was wrong there, but Sloane couldn't figure out what.

And if she didn't figure it out, she'd be letting down her dad. Who'd finally found someone to be with after being so sad and lonely since Sloane's mom died. It felt like a lot to deal with. However, in Sloane's case, she had a dad, two grannies, and a great-granny who would reassure her that, nope, she was actually the best.

However, Amelia's family's idea of "reassuring" was to tell her that, yes, she'd done a terrible job. But not to worry! Because they'd help her keep from doing it again by showing her how to do things better!

Amelia knew this was all a bunch of nonsense. Heck, even her family knew it was a bunch of nonsense. Which was part of the reason they'd all decided to go to family therapy together.

However, *knowing* something isn't true and *feeling* like it isn't true aren't the same thing at all.

Amelia knew she didn't mess everything up all the time.

But she felt like she did.

Sloane listened as Amelia explained all this, her freckled face red and damp with tears. As Amelia pulled her long gloves out of her pocket to wipe at her cheeks, Sloane pointed out, "Yeah, but if you hadn't thrown-up in Jayla Rychner's office, you wouldn't have been able to get a closer look at the map on the wall. Let alone take a picture of it. Getting sick actually helped us!"

Amelia perked up a bit. She hadn't thought about it that way. However, her self-doubt still had its claws in her like a particularly ravenous lion on a gazelle. Immediately, she scowled, "Yeah, but has it actually helped us? *How* has it helped us?"

"Well, we know about the coffin shop. And that Collymore the First probably didn't make a fortune by selling them. And that we need to go to the courthouse. And—Oh!" As she'd been talking, Sloane's phone binged. Out of habit, she took it out and glanced at it.

Mackenzie had posted a new video to TikTok.

And tagged Osburn and Miller-Poe Investigations.

That couldn't be good.

"What?" Amelia demanded, wiping the last of the tears from her face.

"Er, nothing!" Sloane tried to hide her phone, but Amelia snatched it away.

Somehow, Mackenzie had been close by when Amelia got sick from the swings. Worse still, she'd filmed it, posted it, and set it on repeat. As Video Amelia hurled over and over again, disgustingly wet, gushy sounds accompanied it. In large letters, Mac had added, "LOL—these two think they'll make it onto BuzzFeed!"

It already had quite a few likes and reshares already.

Probably mostly the girls on the We Dance Better Than U team.

Who would share it to their friends . . .

And, well, that was how things tended to go viral.

Especially since Amelia's vomiting truly was spectacular. Skye hadn't been wrong when she said that Amelia was better at it than most people.

Tensing up, Sloane waited for her friend's response. Amelia had already been the victim of Mackenzie's social media bullying. And right now, she was feeling especially vulnerable.

Would Amelia be able to handle this?

Sloane couldn't blame her if she couldn't.

Amelia went bright red in the face again. However, her eyes

remained dry. She scowled at Sloane's phone and then tossed it aside.

"Yay," Amelia sighed sarcastically. "I've finally gone viral. It's like a dream come true."

Sloane blinked in surprise and picked up her phone.

"That's it? It doesn't bother you?" she asked.

"*Of course* it bothers me." Amelia shrugged. She pulled out her own phone to make sure she'd cleaned all the tears from her face. "But I don't really care what either her or her mean friends think of me. They're the worst. I care about what *I* think about me."

"That's a very healthy attitude," Sloane replied. "But I don't think I feel as healthy about it."

She snapped her camera into Amelia's selfie stick, turned it on, and held it up so she could talk into the camera. "Mac, it's sad that the only way you can make yourself look good is by tearing other people down. You think we can't solve this case? Well, guess what? We have fifty thousand followers around the world who think we can. Sorry you don't get it the way they do. If you have to post videos making fun of other people to get attention, then I guess we already know that BuzzFeed is never going to give you *your* own show."

She posted it and almost immediately got four likes. Probably from the grannies and the Seifes.

"Did you just go to TikTok war with Mackenzie for me?" Amelia snickered. Feeling more like herself again, she hoisted her parasol onto her shoulder.

"Meh. Whatever." Sloane made a face at her phone. "Let Mackenzie come at me. Oh! It looks like Belinda has sent us something."

As Sloane's phone vibrated with the messages, Amelia's pinged too. She brought it out to check it.

It was a picture of Bunny's tongue.

Their phones pinged again, revealing the tongue again . . .

. . . and then again.

However, the fourth picture that came through was of an old newspaper clipping from a Sandusky County newspaper. It seemed to be from some sort of gossip column.

> **Covington Collymore celebrated his wife Petunia's birthday today by presenting her with a stunning ruby ring. Keen observers might notice that Lettie Lane was buried with an identical-looking ruby ring last autumn in a coffin her family purchased from Collymore. How impressive that he was able to remember it so well that the two rings might be twins! Of course, surely the original is buried with Lettie in the Sandusky County Cemetery.**

Amelia read it twice. Then she said to Sloane, "Is it hinting what I think it's hinting?"

"That Covington Collymore the First stole jewelry from the dead people buried in his coffins?" Sloane asked. "Yup. That's definitely what it's hinting."

Their phones pinged again. A second gossip column appeared, yellowed with age. This one read:

> **Covington and Petunia Collymore celebrated their silver wedding anniversary yesterday. One**

has to wonder how the wealthy Mr. Collymore found so much silver in the coffin-making business. Perhaps he found it *inside* his coffins?

A final text apologized for all the tongue pictures.

Speechless, Sloane and Amelia both shoved their phones away.

They both needed some frozen custard to process this new information.

Five minutes later, ice-cream cones in hand, they walked along the Frontier Trail, discussing what Belinda had sent them.

"Our Covington Collymore *really* isn't going to like hearing that the first Covington Collymore actually made his money as a grave robber," Amelia said between licks as her cone dripped.

Sloane nodded, keeping her own melting ice cream under control. "But it does explain why Collymore the First felt like he couldn't make a big deal about Zistel somehow stealing his land. It sounds like a lot of people in town suspected that Collymore made his own fortune by robbing people. Well, dead people—but still people! I'm sure people didn't like that, so he didn't want to do anything that might make people take a closer look at his old business."

"But he still resented Zistel for swindling him," Amelia continued, sidestepping a creamy splash and abandoning it on the sidewalk for the ants to clean up. "So, he leaves behind the time capsule with the land deed, thinking that his family will understand the clues in the letter. That way, he won't be around for people to hate him for being a grave robber—and his family will still get their land back."

Sloane nodded. "The only problem is, no one understood the clues in his letter."

"Ooo!" Amelia's eyes grew big. "Here's a thought: What if the time capsule he buried doesn't actually have evidence that his land was stolen? He never said that it did in his letter. His wife and kids just assumed that's what he meant. *But what if it has some of those stolen goods hidden inside?*"

Sloane froze.

She hadn't thought of that.

Now she thought about it so long that her cone leaked down her fingers. Frantically, she licked them clean and said, "Maybe that's why Jayla Rychner is hiding the maps from Dr. Jamil. Maybe it isn't that she's trying to keep the time capsule from him. Maybe she's actually hoping he'll find it for her. Maybe *she's* the one pretending to be a ghost and breaking into his office! So she can keep track of his work and swoop in to steal the time capsule the second it's found!"

Of course, they didn't have any proof of this.

It was just a theory.

But there was no denying that Covington Collymore I had been up to no good when he made his fortune.

Coffins, grave robbing, vindictive millionaires, and possibly nefarious park managers.

In spite of her earlier breakdown and Mackenzie's TikTok, Amelia found herself feeling a lot better.

This YouTube video series was going to be a lot more interesting than she had thought just a little bit ago.

What neither she nor Sloane knew, however, was that they had a big problem.

Two big problems, in fact.

Two sparkly, giggly problems.

Following them. Spying on them.

Determined to do more than just ruin their investigation.

Determined to ruin Sloane and Amelia's reputation so thoroughly that no one would ever watch their YouTube channel again.

Nine

Escorted Out

In general, grave-robbing thieves are bad. While buried treasure is usually good. Or at the very least, a better thing than a boring piece of paper. However, if you're a pair of teenage detectives trying to solve a case and make it big on YouTube, these two things can be flip-flopped.

Grave-robbing was horrifying, gross—and sure to get clicks.

"Found treasure" had already been done a bunch of times. Oh, it wasn't *exactly* bad. People would still watch it.

But grave robbing was still more original.

Since the Frontier Trail had a lot of buildings that looked like Ohio in 1875, Sloane filmed Amelia twirling her parasol in front of several of them. Later, Amelia would edit the film together with photographs, old-timey music, and voice-over narration, explaining the case so far.

By the time they finished, Sloane and Amelia had reached a point near the white water rapids ride where the path widened out. A wooden platform stood under the shade of some trees. Hay bales formed rows in front of it. Several exhausted kids and adults lounged on those hay benches. Using battery-operated fans to cool themselves or else trying to dry off their sodden clothes from the watery ride.

A blond woman in a pink Victorian-era dress stood on the stage. She had very pale skin and her dress had a large bustle in back and long ringlets tumbled out from underneath a straw sun bonnet. She held a metal stick in one hand, demonstrating for a group of little kids how to use it to push around a metal hoop. The goal was to keep the hoop upright as it rolled round and round. Off to one side stood a table with a stack of picture books on it. Next to it was a large poster advertising, Dr. Posie Pickerington—children's book author and professor of nineteenth-century American history!

"Dr. Pickerington!" Sloane and Amelia gasped at the same moment.

They sat down on a hay bench to watch.

The preschoolers and kindergarteners each got their own hoop and stick. For a few minutes, they tried spinning their hoops around just like Dr. Pickerington had. However, they quickly realized that it was a lot harder than she'd made it seem.

So then they just whacked each other with their sticks.

As well as their parents.

And anyone else in the audience.

Sloane dodged the thrust of a little girl wielding her stick like a sword.

Amelia snapped her parasol shut and used it to parry a blow from a little boy as he shouted, "Off with your head!"

To everyone's relief, Dr. Pickerington cried, "That's enough!"

She took back her hoops and sticks as all the kids groaned in protest. Her long curls looked frazzled rather than smooth, the way they had on the poster. Sweat sheened her face. She glanced longingly at a nearby fan. Like she wanted nothing more than to hike up her skirts and cool her petticoats in the spinning air.

Collecting herself, Dr. Pickerington gestured toward the colorful stack of picture books. Cartoon characters in suits and stovepipe hats smiled from beneath the balloon-shaped letters of the title: *Super Sandusky and the Men Who Made It Great.* "If you enjoyed my presentation about the past, then I encourage you to purchase a copy of my children's history book! It will teach you all about the honorable, illustrious men who founded the city of Sandusky! And their bravery in establishing a community where before, there was nothing but empty wilderness!"

"Er," said Sloane.

"Uh," muttered Amelia.

Dr. Pickerington's smile froze on her face. In fact, Amelia was pretty sure the professor was actually gnashing her teeth together. In an annoyed-teacher voice, Posie Pickerington asked sweetly, "Yes? Is there something you'd like to say?"

"Well . . ." Amelia scrunched backward into her parasol like it could protect her. "There were people here. You know, the Kaskaskia. The Erie. The Myaamia . . ."

Amelia trailed off as Dr. Pickerington's nostrils flared. The historian put her fists onto her hips. "Well, I'm not talking about *them,* am I? I'm talking about the settlers! Like my great-great-great-great-grandfather, Colonel Pike Pickerington who came here searching for the freedom to make cedar closets. Which he did, opening up Pickerington's Cedar Wardrobes and helping grow the town of Sandusky."

Seeing an opportunity, Sloane decided to jump in. "Speaking

of the settlers, do you know anything about Covington Collymore the First? You know, the gravedigger? The one who made his fortune in coffins?"

That caught everyone's attention. Nothing like mentioning dead bodies to get people interested.

"Are there ghosts in this story?" asked the girl who had almost stabbed Sloane.

"Or zombies?" demanded the boy who had attacked Amelia. "There could be zombies!"

"Dinosaurs!" somebody else said.

"Pirates!" yet another kid suggested. Now they just seemed to be tossing out random things they were interested in. "Ghost pirates! Zombie pirates! Dinosaur pirates! Tell us a story about ghost zombie dinosaurs who become pirates and moved to Sandusky!"

Going rigid, Dr. Pickerington sniffed in outrage. "I'm talking about history! Not made-up stories! None of those things are real!" All the kids went limp with disappointment. Realizing she was losing their interest, Dr. Pickerington glued her smile back onto her face. "That's it for today's presentation! Books are ten dollars each! Learn all about how Colonel Pike Pickerington helped make Sandusky the great town it is today! I'll be right back, if you want one!"

With that, she hitched up her skirts and stormed through the audience to where Sloane and Amelia were sitting. Dr. Pickerington grabbed each of them by the arm and hustled them over behind the restrooms.

"But I don't have to go!" Amelia protested.

Sloane tried to pull her arm free, not at all sure the historian wasn't planning on whacking them with a hoop and a stick once she got them alone. However, Dr. Pickerington was surprisingly strong for someone so dainty. She didn't let go of either one of the girls until they were out of sight of everyone else.

Then she released them and tore off her bonnet. Shaking it, the professor hissed, "Who put you up to this? Was it that quack, Dr. Jamil? I don't know what you're up to, but don't you dare slander my great-great-great-great-grandfather! Or his good friend Covington Collymore. I did my research on every person in that book. There is absolutely no proof that Collymore helped anyone escape from the Sandusky County Jail, let alone Maniac McGee!"

"Wait, *what*?" Amelia gasped. "*Covington Collymore* was the one who helped him escape? Maniac McGee fell out of *his* boat and drowned?"

"It was hardly Covington Collymore's fault that the man slipped!" Dr. Pickerington scrunched her hat in her fists. Then, realizing that she'd pretty much admitted that, yup, Covington Collymore *had* helped Maniac McGee escape, she really lost it. "Is Dr. Jamil paying you to ruin my book? He's just jealous that I got a book deal, and he didn't!"

With that, she stormed off, kicking aside a stray balloon that had escaped a baby's hands. From the stroller, the baby shrieked unhappily as its mother chased after the floating yellow ball, trying to snag its string.

"Sloane, maybe there isn't stolen stuff or a land deed in the time capsule after all!" Amelia cried, lifting up her phone on its selfie stick to show that she'd been secretly filming all along. "Maybe it's Covington Collymore the First's confession that he helped Maniac

McGee escape! Not only would it be a crime, but it accidentally caused the man's death. *He's* the reason Maniac McGee's ghost still haunts Cedar Point. Possibly in the form of a creepy Kewpie doll."

"I don't know, Amelia. That's a lot of leaps in logic," Sloane said uncertainly.

"Okay, so we still don't know what's in the time capsule," Amelia admitted. "But we *do* know that Covington Collymore the First is a lot more interesting than we thought. Coffin-maker, grave robber, and now someone who broke people out of prison—for money, I'm sure."

"Not that he seemed to be very good at it." Sloane made a face. "I mean, if you're going to make money off helping people escape from prison, you also need to be pretty good at keeping them in your boat. I think we need to find out more about Maniac McGee. It might not help us find the time capsule, but I think the people who watch our YouTube channel will want to know his story."

Right about then, both of their phones pinged. They'd been tagged in another video on TikTok.

Both girls pulled it up. Mackenzie had posted a video of Dr. Pickerington screaming at them, followed by the toddler crying in the stroller. Repeated over and over again. Cartoon letters declared, OSBURN AND MILLER-POE INVESTIGATIONS, MAKING LITTLE KIDS CRY!

"How does she keep doing it?" Sloane demanded, swinging around. Trying to spot Mackenzie or CeeCee. She couldn't find anyone who looked even a little bit like their classmate/enemy (clenemy?) or her friend. "How does she always know where we're going to be?"

Amelia didn't know, but she was getting tired of being made to feel weird and ashamed. Throwing away her parasol, she pulled up her own TikTok and yelled into the camera, "Oh yeah? Oh yeah? Well, you're the one who makes little kids cry with your stupid dance moves! Not us! And we didn't even make that kid cry! It was because he lost his balloon—and we didn't do that, either—and—and—"

And fortunately, Sloane took Amelia's phone away before she could actually post it.

"Let's maybe not do that," Sloane said gently. "And I probably shouldn't have posted what I did earlier, either. I think it's probably not a good idea to post *anything* when you're angry."

"Probably not," Amelia admitted, picking up her parasol again. When it hit the ground, it had snapped inside out and didn't want to go back to its normal self again. "Besides, I saw what my hair looked like in the video. Does it really look like that right now?"

The humidity had not done good things to Amelia's curls. She'd tried to tame them into a ladylike bun, but they'd sprung loose.

Like Maniac McGee springing loose from the Sandusky County Jail with Covington Collymore I's help.

Sloane's own ponytail had melted in the heat. It now stuck to her neck and back like it was glued there by the lake air and the sugar from all the cotton candy and slushie machines.

"Let's go take a break back at the hotel room with my grannies," Sloane suggested.

Still struggling with her parasol, Amelia glumly agreed. Sloane reached over and tried to give her a hand, but the parasol appeared to be both smarter and more capable than the two of them combined.

Until they reached the table where Dr. Pickerington was signing copies of her brightly colored children's book. Then, with a mighty shove, Sloane managed to snap the dome back into its proper shape. Unfortunately, the force of it shot the umbrella out of Amelia's hands...

... through the air...

... to bonk the professor on the head.

"Oh no," Amelia squeaked, clapping her hands to her mouth in horror.

Dr. Pickerington wobbled over backward and went down. Her legs flung up into the air, revealing long, lacy pantaloons. The shoes she'd been wearing flew off her feet as she kicked, trying to right herself. However, her many petticoats kept her weighed down.

"Is this part of the show?" a little kid asked uncertainly as several older kids pulled out their phones to film the professor's efforts.

Sloane and Amelia rushed forward to help her.

"I'm so sorry!" Amelia babbled. "It was an accident! You see, it was inside out and the thrust—that's a physics term Mrs. Lemons taught us about in science class—and you see, the thrust—"

The professor, however, was understandably uninterested in anything either Amelia or Sloane had to say. She swatted away their helping hands and grabbed the table to pull herself up onto her feet.

A tower of her books shuddered and then collapsed.

Spilling them into a sticky, pink puddle formed by somebody's melting ice-cream cone.

Ruining them.

"SABOTAGE!" Posie Pickerington shrieked, pointing at Sloane and Amelia.

Who, sensing things were going badly, tried to run. Two security guards caught them, however, before they could make it past the entrance to the white water rapids.

Fifteen minutes later, Sloane and Amelia found themselves back in Jayla Rychner's office. Both Dr. Pickerington and Dr. Jamil were also there. Dr. Pickerington stormed about, throwing her arms up in the air. Dr. Jamil just stood there, giving the maps on Mrs. Rychner's wall the side-eye. He didn't say much, but he was clearly just as annoyed as the other professor.

"He sent those kids to sabotage my event!" The historian pointed at the archaeologist. "He hates that I'm related to Colonel Pike Pickerington! He can't stand that my family is a genuine part of history! If it hadn't been for my great-great-great-great-grandfather's cedar wardrobe factory, Sandusky wouldn't be the great city that it is today!"

That was finally too much for Dr. Jamil.

"What do I care about Colonel Pike Pickerington?" He stopped trying to get a good look at the maps and pointed right back at Dr. Pickerington. "*She* sent those kids to go poking around my dig site, stirring up trouble! I couldn't get my students to focus after they left. All they could talk about were haunted Kewpie dolls and someone called Maniac McGee!"

Just as she had when talking to Sloane and Amelia earlier, Dr. Pickerington went rigid at the mention of his name. "Who Covington Collymore most definitely didn't break out of prison!

People need to stop accusing him of that! He was one of Sandusky's richest and most important citizens!"

Dr. Jamil threw his hands up into the air and gave her a what-are-you-even-talking-about look.

"Why would I care?" he cried, before narrowing his eyes to look at her more closely. "And where were you last night, while my office was being broken into?"

Dr. Pickerington stopped storming around the office. She crossed her arms and her face clamped shut as tightly as an oyster shell. "Don't blame your ghost problems on *me*."

Scoffing at that, Dr. Jamil said, "Ghosts aren't real!"

"Aren't they? I heard that the only thing that appeared on any of the security cameras was an orb of light. Sounds pretty ghostly to me."

"And how do you know that, exactly?" Dr. Jamil demanded. He and Dr. Pickerington had been moving closer and closer to each other. Both with their hands on their hips. "Could you have something to do with it?"

Before an actual brawl could break out, Jayla Rychner stepped in and took charge. "Dr. Pickerington, I apologize for the disaster at your presentation. Dr. Jamil, I likewise apologize for the problems at your archaeological dig. You can rest assured that nothing else will happen today. I will post extra security at the dig tonight. And these two"—she nodded sternly at Sloane and Amelia. Who both tried to look innocent—"will be escorted from the park."

"You can't kick us out!" Sloane protested.

"I can. And I will." Jayla Rychner did just that, snapping her fingers at the two security guards who'd dragged Sloane and Amelia to her office in the first place. "I've already contacted your grandmothers since they're the only adults listed on your park passes. I've got enough problems with the design of our new roller coaster not working out . . . Er, never mind. Everything is fine. Just fine and dandy. Absolutely fine and dandy—"

A crash from outside the building interrupted the park manager.

Jayla Rychner bolted from the room, followed by the guards, dragging Sloane and Amelia along with them.

Earlier in the day, the test car for the Master of Mayhem kept shaking as it went up the half-finished hill. Shaking and threatening to tip over.

It was no longer threatening.

Instead, it lay on the ground in a heap of twisted metal and shattered fiberglass.

Amelia went woozy. Grabbing Sloane for support, she gasped, "I've had nightmares about being on a ride when that happens."

Not surprisingly, Jayla Rychner wasn't exactly pleased to hear that.

"Get them out of here!" She snapped her fingers at the guards before rushing forward to deal with the construction and crew and designers.

The other park guests watched them go, whispering to each other and trying to figure out what two kids could have done to get thrown out. Sloane marched with her head held high, refusing to give anyone the satisfaction of seeing her look ashamed. Amelia hunched over and hid beneath the protective shell of her parasol.

At the exit, the grannies and the two Seife kids waited for them. Granny Kitty and Granny Pearl had on their serious faces but gave both Sloane and Amelia fierce hugs.

Skye announced to the security guards, "If you're going to throw out Amelia, then you're going to have to throw out me too!"

"You're already outside the park, kid." One of the guards rolled his eyes.

Skye thought it over and then ducked under the turnstile to return to the park.

Once there, she wrapped her arms and legs around a bench and refused to let go.

Brighton, who knew his sister, shook his head."He shouldn't have said that. This is probably going to be a while."

As he took out his phone to see if he could find any Poké Balls, another security guard left the station at the exit. The door took a moment to fall shut again, and in that time, Amelia spotted several large computer monitors inside.

Showing the views from various security cameras.

Including one pointing right at the dig.

"Sloane!" She nudged her friend with her elbow. Sloane followed her gaze as Amelia whispered, "If we could just take a look at it, I bet we could see that orb at the dig!"

Unfortunately, the security guards had already managed to pry Skye's feet from the bench. She still had a pretty good grip on the armrest, but Sloane wasn't sure it would give them enough time to look at the camera.

She turned to her grannies. "Uh, Granny Pearl and Granny Kitty—"

The two grannies had already heard what Amelia said. They might not know anything about any mysterious orb, but they were always up for a little mischief.

"On it!" Granny Kitty said as Granny Pearl gave them a wink.

Sloane and Amelia slipped into the security booth, being sure to leave the door propped open for an easy escape.

Amelia collapsed her parasol and sat down in the wheeled chair. "This looks a lot like the program my parents use for the security cameras outside our house."

"Your house has security cameras?"

"Everyone in our neighborhood does." Amelia rolled her eyes. "They're all convinced that robbers could be coming after their things at any moment. But our camera only ever records deer, raccoons, and the Meeker kids next door, sneaking through our yard."

Grabbing the mouse, she clicked on the camera showing the dig. It expanded to fill the monitor. Then Amelia grabbed the little tab on the timeline and dragged it backward. Everything on the screen moved quickly in reverse, day giving way to night.

Until a large, oblong orb bounced onto the screen.

Even expecting it, both Sloane and Amelia gasped in surprise.

The orb moved about the dig, opening a large storage box and throwing about the tools inside. Then it pulled up some of the wooden marking stakes and tangled up the strings attached, ruining the grid. Finally, it disappeared into Dr. Jamil's office for a few minutes, before coming back out and vanishing into the night.

"Huh." Sloane twisted the tip of her ponytail around her fingertip. "That orb was definitely as big as an adult."

"Or at least a teenager," Amelia agreed.

Through the propped-open door, Skye's wailing drew closer. A grim-faced guard carried her, kicking and screaming. He seemed to be regretting every choice he ever made that had brought him to this moment in his life.

He was about to have even more regrets.

Granny Pearl fell to the ground, shrieking, "My sciatica! My sciatica! Oh, help! Help!"

Standing over her, Granny Kitty clapped her hands to either side of her face and wailed, "Will no one help a poor, elderly woman?"

Everyone rushed forward. When the guard carrying Skye set her down, the little girl scurried back under the turnstile and wrapped herself around the bench once more.

Brighton looked it all over, shook his head, and returned to his Pokémon game.

"That should buy us another minute." Sloane turned her attention back to the security cameras. "Can you check any of the other cameras in the park? Can we see where the orb came from? And where it went?"

Amelia quickly checked a few of the surrounding cameras. She followed its path backward through the park.

It hadn't come out of Lake Erie.

It had climbed over the chain-link fence from the parking lot.

Unless the ghost of Maniac McGee drove a car, the orb was somehow human.

Ten

Maniac McGee

In theory, you can't say for sure that ghosts don't drive cars.

Of course, that's because you can't say for sure that ghosts do—or don't do—anything at all.

Mostly because it's impossible to say for sure that ghosts exist.

(How much most people believe in ghosts vary. They typically believe in them more when they're alone in the dark and have just heard a weird sound.)

Who was behind the glowing orb, neither Sloane nor Amelia could say.

But they were both confident that it had something to do with Collymore's lost time capsule.

Granny Pearl's sciatica attack had mysteriously vanished as soon as Sloane and Amelia slipped out of the guard booth. At that point, she'd promptly jumped to her feet, nimble as ever. Amelia convinced Skye to release the bench, and everyone had hurried away before an ambulance could be called or anyone could figure out what sciatica was.

Granny Kitty and Granny Pearl agreed to go to the Sandusky County Courthouse—as soon as they'd taken Skye and Brighton to the beach. Sloane and Amelia protested at this delay, but the grannies pointed out that they'd agreed to do that before Sloane and

Amelia asked for help. Since the courthouse didn't close until five o'clock and it was only three o'clock, Granny Pearl and Granny Kitty swore there was enough time to give everyone what they wanted.

Neither Sloane nor Amelia were sure about that.

However, as neither was old enough to drive, let alone actually own a car, they had no choice but to go along with the plan.

So, a little later, Sloane and Amelia lounged in beach chairs overlooking the silvery, shimmering waves of Lake Erie. Puffy white clouds scuttled across the deep blue sky as though trying to escape the caws of the seagulls wheeling beneath them.

Brighton and Skye worked on building a sandcastle, while Granny Kitty and Granny Pearl relaxed in a nearby cabana. While they wore normal swimsuits, Amelia wore one from the 1880s: a frilly cap, a dress, puffy pants that fell to her knees, and long stockings with ballet flats.

Skye had gazed at her wistfully.

"I want a bathing suit just like that for my birthday," she sighed before returning to her sandcastle. "And one for Bertram Cordelia too."

The concrete goose wore a pink polka-dot bikini, straw hat, and sunglasses as it sat in its wagon, nearby in the sand.

"I've never had a fan before," Amelia said to Sloane. She had her tablet in her hands so she could start editing the video they had shot at the park.

"I think she might actually be more of a stalker." Skye's dedication to Amelia was both adorable and a little scary.

"Well, I've never had one of those before either."

"You might want to get used to it." Sloane checked their TikTok profile. "We've actually gained over a thousand followers since this morning."

"I think it might be because of the videos that Mackenzie keeps posting." Amelia snickered, leaning over to look. "Look, every time she makes fun of us, people actually check out our TikTok. Then they're linking to our YouTube and watching our investigations into the Hoäl Jewels and Ma Yaklin's Missing Millions. Our YouTube subscribers are up too."

Sloane turned on her video recorder. "Here, let's make a video thanking her."

Amelia leaned into view. "Hey, Mackenzie! Thank you *so much* for all your kind words!"

Grinning, Sloane added, "We'd never get deals with BuzzFeed and Apple TV without you! You're the best, Mac!"

Amelia blew a kiss at the camera. "Love you!"

With a laugh, Sloane tagged Mackenzie and uploaded the video to TikTok. "Ha. If that doesn't make her tear out her hair bow, nothing will."

From over by the sandcastle, Brighton squinted at them. "Do you guys really have deals with BuzzFeed and Apple TV?"

For once, he didn't look at Sloane with suspicion or disgust. So, she really hated to admit, "Well . . . no. I mean, not exactly. It's sort of a joke."

"But we *are* the number-one-most-watched YouTube series in the category of cold case historical investigations by anyone under the age of eighteen, though!" Amelia bragged, looking up from her tablet.

"Oh." Still squinting into the sun, Brighton considered this.

"How many other YouTubers do that sort of thing?"

"That's not the point."

"Oh." Brighton didn't say anything else. But Sloane sort of got the sense that he thought it *was* the point.

He returned to helping Skye with the sandcastle. The two of them waded in the foam, looking for shells to form doors and windows.

"Why can't I get that kid to like me?" Sloane asked while her friend deleted bits of the film, while moving other chunks around the time line.

"Hm." Amelia paused what she was doing to thoughtfully tap her lower lip with her fingertip. "I dunno, but remember how you felt about the Seifes when your dad first started dating Cynthia? Like, it can be pretty overwhelming to suddenly have a new family, right?"

"Yeah, but I got over it already," Sloane pointed out grouchily.

Amelia shrugged. "So, it's taking Brighton a little longer, that's all."

"He's smaller. It shouldn't take as long!"

Before Sloane could say anything else, a bucketful of sand hit her in the face.

"BLECH! YUCK!" Letting her tablet fall into her lap, Amelia wiped away the grit with both hands. Then spit out more grains that had found their way into her mouth. "What the what?"

"Oops. Sorry." Mackenzie smiled evilly, a plastic bucket in her hands.

CeeCee joined her. "We were trying to build a sandcastle. Guess the wind caught it."

The two of them wore black and silver bathing suits with matching silver flip-flops. CeeCee held up her phone, clearly filming Amelia. Who was still scraping the sand from her tongue.

Sloane lifted up her sunglasses to scowl at them both. "Yeah, I guess. I bet that's why you had your phone out to record it, huh?"

Collymore's daughter didn't look the least bit ashamed. "I was just trying to take a picture of your friend's weird outfit. What even *is* that?"

Amelia gave up on the sand and decided to just swallow the rest. Hotly, she said, "*That* is an authentic 1880s swimsuit! And I've noticed that lots of people on your TikTok like my costumes."

Mackenzie and CeeCee looked at each other. Then they burst out laughing like Amelia's comment was the funniest thing they'd ever heard.

"Oh, so you follow our TikTok, huh?" Mackenzie sneered. "I knew it!"

Amelia felt herself blushing and hated herself for it. Why could Mackenzie always get under her skin like that? *Of course* she checked their TikTok! Just like Mackenzie clearly followed all the social media accounts run by Osburn and Miller-Poe Investigations. How could she make Amelia feel like she'd done something stupid with one look, one laugh, and one "I knew it!"

Sloane had given up on trying to make Mackenzie feel embarrassed. Ignoring the girl, Sloane turned to CeeCee. "I get why Mac is giving us a hard time. I mean, not only is she the worst, she's also clearly super jealous of us. What I don't get, is why are *you* helping her? Your dad is the one who hired us, and if we find that time capsule, it could make him a lot of money."

CeeCee's face went stony as the wind whipped her ponytail around her face. Her hands clenched into fists. "What do I care about some stupid money? We're already super rich. He needs to get over it and worry more about my dance competition than some farm somebody owned, like, a billion years ago."

There was no mistaking the bitterness in her voice.

There was also no mistaking the fact that Brighton and Skye were sneaking up on Mackenzie and CeeCee.

With a bucket of something silvery.

And stinky.

The wind carried the smell over to the two girls just in time to make them gag and turn around.

But not soon enough to avoid the pailful of rotten fish that Brighton and Skye flung at them.

"That is so gross!" Mackenzie screeched, slapping the smelly, squishy fish from her bathing suit and legs. CeeCee likewise hopped backward, screaming.

The trouble of it was, even once they kicked and knocked the fish away, the stench still clung to them. Sloane and Amelia both pinched their noses shut as they laughed.

"Sorry," Skye said, not actually sounding even a little bit sorry.

"The wind must have caught it," Brighton said, throwing their excuse back at the two mean girls. Sloane looked at him in surprise. Brighton gave her a half smile in return, then seemed to think he was being too friendly and turned away.

Right about then, Grandma Synder stormed down the board-walk and out onto the beach. She wore a loose, silver-and-black dress, and she was not happy with the Seife kids. Granny Kitty and

Granny Pearl quickly jumped to the little kids' defense. Several angry words were exchanged, with Grandma Snyder finally spitting out, "Oh, go stick your bingo card where the sun doesn't shine! Which is your garden, given how sad and mangy all your flowers look!"

She hustled away her granddaughter and friend while the two grannies were sputtering in outrage.

"Oh, she's just lucky we don't set Nanna Tia on her!" Granny Kitty gasped, while Granny Pearl furiously gathered up their beach bags and towels.

"Don't worry, Kitty. We'll fix her after we go to the courthouse for Sloane-y and Amelia. Once they get a deal with BuzzFeed or Apple TV, those Snyders won't be laughing anymore."

"Oh. That's all just kind of a joke," Sloane explained awkwardly as she and Amelia helped load the plastic buckets and shovels into the wagon next to Bertram Cordelia. Er, Cordelia.

"It isn't, though." Granny Kitty pulled out her phone and showed it to her granddaughter. "See, they're both following you now on YouTube."

Amelia grabbed the phone and shoved it to her face. Like she was so excited, she was trying to climb into the phone itself. "She's right! See, Sloane? *See?* I told you that, if you convince enough people of a thing, you can actually make it happen!"

Though her heart was fluttering with excitement, Sloane played it cool. "Following us doesn't mean either one of them is going to offer us a deal."

Waving a dismissive hand, Amelia kept her face buried in the phone the entire way across the beach and up the boardwalk to the hotel. Granny Kitty finally had to pry it out of Amelia's fingers. Leaving Amelia with a dreamy smile on her face as she continued to mumble, "BuzzFeed! Apple TV!" over and over again.

For obvious reasons, neither Skye nor Brighton wanted to go to the courthouse with the two grannies. While Amelia went up to their hotel suite to continue putting together the first video in their series on The Quandary of the Collymore Capsule, Sloane hung out with the two little kids at the hotel pool. By the time they'd all had enough sun, water, and chlorine, the two grannies still weren't back from the courthouse. Sloane took the Seifes upstairs to find Amelia with a pair of headphones jammed over her ears, feverishly cutting and pasting video clips together with photographs of Cedar Point back in the late 1800s and early 1900s.

Everyone else took turns using the shower. With everyone clean, the grannies *still* weren't back. Sloane sent them a text message, but the only thing she got back was, "Working on it." With a shrug, she ordered three pizzas—one cheese for the Seifes, one with tomato and olives for Amelia, and one with bacon and banana peppers for herself. When they arrived, Sloane tried to pull the headphones off Amelia's head and drag her away from her tablet. Only to have Amelia grip the edge of the desk and shout, "I'm not done! You can't rush great art!"

Giving up, Sloane shoved a slice of pizza into her friend's hand and joined Brighton and Skye on the couch as they watched TV, played games on their tablets, and tried to feed pizza to Bertram Cordelia.

With the Seifes distracted, Sloane researched Maniac McGee. She found a few websites about ghosts and hauntings at Cedar Point.

A couple mentioned his name and called him an escaped prisoner who drowned in Lake Erie, but that was pretty much it—well, other than the fact that he supposedly roamed the beaches at midnight.

Finally, fourth slice of pizza in hand, she found a link to the Sandusky County Historical Society. It was from last Halloween, and it was all about ghosts at Cedar Point, too:

> One of the better-known ghosts at the amusement park is Maniac McGee. Each year, visitors thrill to stories of how he wanders along the shoreline. Beckoning guests to follow him into Lake Erie and a watery grave. Actors dressed as a ghostly version of McGee tell how he drowned while escaping from the county jail. What people might not know is that Murdock "Maniac" McGee was a real person. According to the **Sandusky County Recorder** newspaper, on August 1, 1875, he arrived in town, "having become massively rich out West when he discovered a gold mine." McGee checked into the fanciest hotel in town. Unfortunately, once there, he seemed to still think he was in the Wild West. According to the *Recorder*, "On August 2, Mr. McGee took offense to a song being played on the piano in the dining room. He took out a pair of pistols and filled the piano with enough holes to make it look like Swiss cheese. Mr. McGee was arrested and charged with disturbing the peace and destruction of property." Rather than

wait for his trial, McGee broke out of prison. Since the railroads were on alert for escaped prisoners, he tried to escape across Lake Erie to Canada. Unfortunately, a summer thunderstorm had made the waves choppy. McGee fell overboard and drowned, quickly going from one of the luckiest men in Ohio to one of the unluckiest. Rumor has it that someone may have helped McGee to escape, but no one was ever charged with that crime.

Hmmm...

This seemed to confirm what Dr. Posie Pickerington had said earlier in the day.

In his letter, Collymore I said that the events of 1875 "weighed heavily upon my mind." Collymore VI assumed that it had to be because Zistel stole his whatever-many-great-grandpa's land.

It was looking more and more like Collymore I meant— whoops!—being good at breaking McGee out of prison, but very bad at keeping him alive afterward.

Surfacing up out of her internet wormhole, Sloane found Amelia stumbling out of their room with bleary eyes. She had uploaded their latest YouTube video, she informed Sloane as she crammed a slice of pizza into her mouth.

"Where are Granny Kitty and Granny Pearl?" she mumbled around a mouthful of tomato and olive.

Sloane checked her phone. "They texted me ten minutes ago, saying they're on their way back and will be here in twenty minutes. I wonder what they found?"

"That can wait. The park has been closed for an hour. We should really go poke around before your grannies get back and tell us we can't. You know, just outside around the chain-link fence. Near where we saw that orb go over it." Amelia pretended like this idea had just occurred to her. Even though it was super clear to Sloane that Amelia had been planning this for hours.

"Well . . ." Sloane hesitated. True, they'd been thrown out of the park. But Amelia wasn't talking about actually going *into* the park. Just walking around near it.

Having heard Amelia, Brighton lifted his head up from his Pokémon game. "Wait—what? You're leaving us? What if Granny Kitty and Granny Pearl *aren't* back in ten minutes? What if any ghosts try to break in?"

He sounded pretty anxious about it, dropping his tablet and twisting his fingers together. Sloane pulled out her phone and checked her Find Friends app. The grannies were out in the parking lot and would be back to the hotel room any moment now.

"Locked doors keep out ghosts," Sloane promised him. "The grannies are downstairs. Just don't open the door to anyone except them."

This didn't reassure Brighton. In fact, it seemed to do the opposite. He jumped up from the couch and yelled, "I knew you'd do this! I knew you'd leave us the second you got the chance!"

Sloane blinked in surprise. Then it hit her.

The reason Brighton kept pushing her away. The reason, actually, that he really didn't talk much to the grannies, either. Or—come to think of it—even Sloane's dad.

He was afraid of losing them. Of being left behind.

Of growing to care for Sloane, her dad, and the grannies.

Only to watch them leave.

Just like he felt like his dad had.

"Oh, Brighton," Sloane began. "That's not what's happening."

But Brighton didn't want to hear it. He ran into the bathroom and slammed the door shut. When Sloane knocked on it, he yelled, "I need my privacy! Bathrooms are for privacy!"

Sloane stood helplessly on the other side of the door, not knowing what to say or do. Which, she should—so why didn't she? Sloane had lost her mom in a way Brighton hadn't lost his dad. Sure, his dad had moved out of their house, and they didn't get to see him nearly as much anymore. But at least they *did* get to see him. Plus, they could FaceTime whenever they wanted!

Both of which were things Sloane would never again get to do with *her* mom.

Resentment grew in Sloane's stomach. Hot, blistery, acidy resentment. What did it matter that Brighton was practically half her age? She should be the one anxious about losing more people, not him! *She* should be the one acting all cold toward him—not the other way around!

"Fine! Stay in the bathroom and have all the privacy you want!" Sloane huffed. She stomped into the living room, expecting to find Amelia in her black cat burglar outfit and vent to her.

She did find Amelia.

However, the second Sloane laid eyes on her friend, she forgot all about Brighton and venting.

Because Amelia wasn't wearing her black cat burglar outfit.

Instead, she wore a clown costume.

Frilly collar. Baggy jumpsuit.

Peaked hat.

"No," Sloane whispered. Clearing her voice, she said more clearly. "Amelia, no."

"But we need disguises! What if there are clown ghosts wandering around near the park?" Amelia waved a curly wig and red nose at her friend. "We'll want to blend in with them, if that happens! They won't attack us if they think we're clown ghosts too!"

Sloane smacked a hand to her face, trying to think of something that would talk her friend out of this.

She couldn't think of a single thing. Not knowing Amelia, anyhow. She could think of about a hundred reasons that would convince anyone else.

But not Amelia.

The best Sloane could do was refuse the wig and the nose. "Fine. You wear that. But I'm not wearing *those*."

"But what about the ghost clowns?"

"Just tell them I'm with you."

Since Sloane didn't want them, Skye happily claimed the wig and nose. She popped the red ball onto her own nose and tugged the wig over her purple bow and ponytail. Her brother was still shut in the bathroom, but Sloane didn't care.

She left with Amelia

To find a ghost or to find a person.

And to hopefully find more clues to where Collymore's time capsule might be buried.

Eleven

Ghost clowns are a sensible thing to be afraid of when breaking into an amusement park after dark.

Breaking into anything is a terrible idea. Partly because it's illegal.

And partly because there might be ghost clowns.

True, you don't hear a lot about people being carried off by ghost clowns after breaking into amusement parks. But then you wouldn't.

Because those people would never come back.

Regardless, Sloane and Amelia used the stairs rather than the elevator to avoid running into the grannies and being told to get back up to their hotel room. They encountered a few other people, with the adults tending to chuckle at Amelia's clown outfit. While the kids usually stepped back in terror.

Personally, Sloane thought the kids were smarter than the adults.

Night had swept in from the lake, plunging the parking lot into inky darkness. Streetlamps patterned the sky, casting enough hazy light to block out the stars above. Mayflies swirled round and round the globes, hypnotized. With the sun gone, the breeze stirred away the humidity, leaving Sloane to shiver and wish she'd brought a hoodie.

On the other side of the parking lot, little log cabins clustered around an old stone lighthouse. The cabins were for "camping," though Sloane didn't see how it could really be camping if you weren't in a sleeping bag on the ground inside a tent. Which was what her dad and Cynthia Seife wanted both families to do together before the summer was over. Go camping down in Hocking Hills, Ohio.

Which . . . Sloane liked being outside and hiking.

She was less thrilled about sleeping in an uncomfortable sleeping bag rather than her own, nice, comfy bed.

She was even *less* sure about dragging a concrete goose up and down the trails in a wagon.

Sloane and Amelia melted into the shadows and tiptoed toward the park, walking along the fence. They didn't want to draw the attention of any night watchmen who might be patrolling it from the other side. In the video footage from the security booth, Sloane had noticed a sign that said B8. The parking lot had signs like that, labeling different parts of it to help people find their cars again. Even though the day had ended, all the lights in the lot remained on. Eerie orange light trickled down from their tall, pale posts as the night breeze helped a mist creep in from the lake. The fog must roll in fairly frequently, for the location signs were posted high enough that they could still be seen above it.

Amelia shivered and wrapped her baggy clown suit more closely around her chest. "Those streetlights look exactly like bony fingers poking up out of the ground."

Her words made Sloane's hair stand on end. "Please don't say things like that, okay?"

Shrugging, Amelia did as Sloane asked. However, she took out her phone so she could film the fog as it grew thicker and thicker. Rising up to swallow first the signs and then the lights themselves. Ever hungry, it continued past Sloane and Amelia to gobble up the park itself.

Fortunately, by then, the two girls had found the area of the chain link fence closest to the B8 parking lot sign. They sunk down into the swirling mist, hidden by a sign that proclaimed, WELCOME TO CEDAR POINT!

From there the two girls didn't have much to do other than wait, hope the "ghost" showed up and led them to something useful in their search for Collymore's lost time capsule. Or at the very least, did something that would make for an interesting episode in their YouTube series.

Both real and fake ghosts could be counted on to do that.

The time stamp on the security camera footage had shown that the intruder went over the park fence around 12:30 a.m. Since that was the person leaving, it seemed reasonable that they'd entered the park around 12:15, to give them enough time to trash the dig site and break into Dr. Jamil's office.

Sloane and Amelia squatted down behind the sign around 11:45, which meant they had a lot of time to kill. Without their phones, since they couldn't risk the light being seen—not even with the cover of the fog.

They couldn't really talk, either, without the chance of being heard.

So, they tried playing rock, paper, scissors.

Which was interesting for about five minutes.

After that, they just sat there.

With the cold and the damp slowly sinking into their butts.

Realizing that this must have been what it was like to entertain yourself before there were phones and tablets.

It was horrifyingly boring.

Twelve fifteen came and went. As did twelve thirty.

With twelve forty-five looming up on them, Amelia couldn't take it anymore. Her legs ached, her right foot had gone to sleep, and the chill rising up off the grass had finally crept its way up to her shoulders and settled there. Just as she stood up and opened her mouth to say, *Let's go home,* something finally happened.

A figure formed out of the mist.

Amelia clapped a hand over her mouth to keep a frightened squeak from escaping. Sloane yanked her back down into the grass again. They both pressed themselves flat into the dew, hearts pounding as they prayed they hadn't been seen.

The figure paused, appearing to stare where Amelia's peaked clown's hat had recently been sticking out into the mist.

Whoever it was shook their head, apparently deciding that they couldn't possibly have seen a clown hat. That it must have been some trick of the darkness.

They turned their attention to the fence.

The person wore some sort of strange bodysuit. It was tight and black, with a hood pulled low over the person's forehead. A black mask covered the person's mouth and nose, with a pair of strange goggles also hiding their eyes. Altogether, it was impossible to see a single distinguishing feature about them. From their placement on the ground, it was even difficult for Sloane or Amelia to say how tall the person was since everything was taller than either one of them from that angle.

And that was before the person pressed some sort of button on the chest of their bodysuit.

Instantly, a pattern of small LED bulbs lit up all over it.

They hiked an athletic shoe into the chain-link fence, and then climbed up and over it.

Landing in the soft gravel on the other side, the hooded person took off into the park.

Getting up, Sloane rubbed at her eyes. She'd been staring right at the suit when it lit up. Now phantom lights danced in front of her vision.

"What was that all about?" she asked Amelia.

"Keep your voice down!" Amelia warned as she stood up and ran over to the fence. "Whoever it is, they are using those LED lights to trick the security camera! On video, all those lights blur together into one, big light."

She held up her phone to show her friend.

Amelia was right. On video, the person glowed like a giant orb.

"Come on! They're getting away!" Amelia shoved a mask, red nose, and clown hat into Sloane's hands.

"Amelia, I already told you! I'm not wearing those!"

"You will if you don't want to be recognized on the security camera," Amelia pointed out smugly.

Sloane froze.

Smacked a hand to her face.

And put on the disguise.

Together, they went up and over the chain-link fence.

The fog prevented them from seeing the hooded person anymore. However, Sloane and Amelia knew the general direction the person had gone: the archaeological dig over by the Coliseum. The biggest challenge was getting there without running into anything: bushes, trees, benches.

Security guards.

As they reached the causeway, Sloane and Amelia almost smacked right into one. If it hadn't been for the fog, the two of them would have been spotted for sure. As it was, Sloane snagged Amelia by the frilly collar and dragged her behind the entrance for the cable cars dangling overhead.

The security guard swung her flashlight around, but it bounced off the mist. Any movements Sloane and Amelia had made were lost in the swirl of damp lake air.

After a moment, the guard and her light moved reluctantly away.

"I bet Jayla Rychner has posted extra guards around the dig," Sloane grumbled.

At least the other intruder had to avoid the guards as well. In spite of a head start, the person hadn't actually made it into the roped-off dig area. As Sloane and Amelia poked their heads out from behind the cable car entrance, the suit lit up again, just across the causeway.

"They must turn their suit lights on and off!" Amelia realized as they darted after the person. "Depending on whether they need to fool the cameras or hide from the guards!"

Reaching the yellow caution tape, they ducked underneath it.

Up ahead of them, the intruder wasn't bothering with messing up the dig site this time. Instead, the person went straight into the dig office. As Sloane and Amelia watched, the person took out a plastic key card and used it to swipe their way inside. The lock turned green, allowing the person inside.

Sloane and Amelia hurried after them.

Only for Sloane to almost fall into one of the excavated holes. She managed to keep her balance, but Amelia wasn't so lucky.

She went down into a separate hole.

"Sloane! Help! I think there's another Kewpie doll down in here with me!" she gasped.

As Sloane bent over to assist her friend, the office door swung open again. Whatever the fake ghost had been looking for, they'd found it much faster this time. The hooded figure bounded out the door, just as a voice out on the causeway yelled, "Hey, Frankie! I think there's someone over by the dig!"

"We've got to get out of here!" Sloane tried to pull Amelia out of the hole, but the loose dirt at the edge gave way.

Sloane tumbled into the hole as well.

Heels pounded toward them from the office—the fake ghost trying to escape. Sloane clawed her way to her feet. If she and Amelia were caught, then her dad would get a phone call that his daughter had committed a felony. If that happened, then there was no way Sloane was going to let the two of them take the blame alone. Peering over the edge of the hole and into the murk, she saw the figure running toward them.

She snagged them by the ankle.

The "ghost" fell with a thud.

With a smaller thud following.

Something bounced into the hole along with the phantom.

As Sloane grappled with the mystery burglar, Amelia felt around. First, her fingers encountered jagged, porcelain shards. Gah! The Kewpie doll, the Kewpie doll!

The ghost kicked at Sloane, flinging her backward and into Amelia. Causing her to eat dirt once again.

"Sorry!" Sloane gritted, refusing to let go.

If Sloane was determined, so were the guards. Out on the causeway, Frankie shouted, "Come on, Devin! We've got him this time, for sure!"

A sharp pain had stabbed through Amelia's fingers when she accidentally grabbed the broken Kewpie doll. However, if everyone else could be determined in the face of danger, then so could she. Ducking under the thrashing legs of the ghost—and avoiding Sloane as those legs flung her about—Amelia found the object.

It was a book!

A book?

Amelia didn't have time to wonder about it. She shoved it inside her baggy clown suit.

The ghost finally managed to kick free of Sloane. The person bounded out of the hole and then off into the fog as the voices of Frankie and Devin drew closer. "Over there! I see some lights!"

"It's the ghost, Frankie! It's the ghost! *It's Maniac McGee!*" Devin sounded like he might very well have peed his paints in terror.

Amelia couldn't blame him. After realizing she was in a

grave-like pit with a Kewpie doll, she was looking forward to changing her clothes too.

Sloane might have lost her grip on the intruder, but she finally managed to scramble her way up and out of the hole. "Come on!"

Fear—of Kewpie dolls and of getting caught—gave Amelia the ability to shoot out of the hole just as quickly.

"Don't be like that, Devin!" Frankie called. From nearby it seemed. Though fog could do strange things to both light and sound. "You go check out the dig. I'll try to find whatever that was."

The rustle of plastic tape told Sloane and Amelia that the frightened Devin was coming closer to them. In a shaky voice, he cried, "H-Hey! Wh-whoever's there, you'd better come out!"

Sloane and Amelia turned to run.

Only to almost slide into another dig hole.

They caught themselves in time.

But so did Devin.

Amelia shrieked as he grabbed her by the clown costume and swung her around. Face-to-face, he didn't look much older than eighteen. Devin took in her clown outfit and released her, letting out a shriek to match Amelia's.

"FRANKIEEEEE!!! It's a clown ghost! *A clown ghost!*"

Sloane seized Amelia by the hand and pulled her away into the mist. Devin quickly disappeared behind them, erased by billows of white. Since they'd already been sort of busted anyhow, both girls turned on their phones' flashlights. Now able to see, they could avoid the rest of the dig's holes until they finally reached the orange, plastic fencing on the other side. They leaped over it as shoes pounded behind them.

Devin was still babbling about ghosts, but Frankie wasn't.

She seemed determined to catch up to them.

They'd come out of the dig on the opposite side from the rest of the park. If they wanted to disappear into it, they'd have to get around the too-determined Frankie.

"We'll never do it!" Amelia gasped.

Feeling that her friend was right, Sloane jerked her head toward the Master of Mayhem. They couldn't see it in the fog, but Sloane knew that the boardwalk and lake had to be on the other side of it. "That way! We can go over the fence and onto the beach!"

Between the shadows and the fog, they hoped to ditch Frankie. Clambering over the plastic fencing, they ran through the construction site. Bulldozers and cranes made strange, threatening animals in the fog, while the half-built first hill loomed over them.

Like the jaws of some hungry beast. Eager to devour them.

Amelia squeaked in terror, and even Sloane felt a shiver running down her spine.

The Master of Mayhem was like a skeleton roller coaster. An undead roller coaster. An evil, dangerous . . .

"Devin, I think they're in the construction site!" A light pierced the fog and swung toward Sloane and Amelia, as they clung to each other, frozen in place by the bones of the coaster above them.

Shaking herself, Sloane pushed Amelia forward and out of the way just in time. The light swung past them and was lost again in the fog.

They raced through the rest of the construction site, hopped the fence, and landed into soft sand and prickly weeds.

"Take off your shoes," Sloane hissed, doing exactly that. "We can run faster on the wet sand closer to the lake."

Amelia followed suit. Carrying their shoes and socks, they ran until they felt cold water under the soles of their feet. Turning to their left, they raced toward the Breakers Hotel. Frankie's voice continued behind them.

Sometimes farther away . . .

. . . sometimes practically on top of them.

A trick of the fog? Or reality?

Ahead of Sloane and Amelia, the mist glowed like a huge lantern had been set down before them. The hotel! The two of them swung toward it, wet sand giving way to dry—and then to the concrete of one of the hotel's many walkways.

They'd made it!

Sloane and Amelia pounded toward a side door, their damp feet slapping against the pavement.

When a shadow rose up out of the fog.

And grabbed them.

Twelve

Why It's Important to Read Source Materials

After breaking into an amusement park and then being attacked, it would be sensible to assume that you're dealing with ghost clowns. After all, they are the most likely creatures to attack someone who's been foolish enough to do such a thing.

However, in Sloane and Amelia's case, the list of possible suspects was actually quite long.

The ghost of Maniac McGee.

The ghost of the Kewpie doll.

Jayla Rychner.

The guards.

For the next several seconds, it was hard to tell who, exactly, had attacked Sloane and Amelia. Or what was going on. The shadow split apart into several shadows, two of them apparently holding clubs. Much shrieking, kicking, and slapping occurred. But after a few seconds, both Sloane and Amelia realized that only some of the shrieking was coming from the two of them.

Then a lake breeze stirred the air, allowing light from a nearby lamp to pierce the fog.

Revealing their attackers to be none other than Granny Kitty, Granny Pearl, Brighton, and Skye.

Everyone said, "What are you doing here?"

Granny Kitty pulled on her glasses so she could get a better look at her granddaughter and her friend. "Sloane-y, why are you dressed as a clown?"

Brighton cut in. "We thought you were ghost clowns come to murder us."

"No, it's only the Kewpie dolls you have to worry about doing that," Amelia assured him as she stripped off her now-damp mask, peaked hat, and baggy clown suit. Underneath, she clutched the book she'd found and wore a perfectly normal tank top and pair of leggings. Well, normal for anyone who wasn't Amelia.

Sloane had questions of her own. As she tore off her own clown nose and hat, she asked suspiciously, "Hey, why are you carrying shovels?"

The grannies instantly looked shifty. No amount of fog could cover up that fact. They whipped the shovels behind their backs.

Then tried to tuck the two Seife kids behind them as well.

Because the two younger kids were each carrying a rosebush.

Dirt still clinging to the roots.

"Grannies, you can't keep stealing other people's flowers for your gardens!" Sloane cried, clapping a hand to either side of her head in horror. "They'll kick us out and never let us come back!"

"Plus, it's wrong," Amelia pointed out. "Like, morally speaking. You know, in terms of right and wrong?"

Sloane blinked rapidly. Wow. She'd almost forgotten about that.

Granny Pearl patted Sloane reassuringly as she and Granny Kitty shepherded everyone toward the side door. "And what will they do, Sloane-y, if they find out the two of you were trespassing in the park, hmm?"

Amelia answered for her friend. In a small voice, she admitted, "Oh. They'd probably think that was wrong too."

Over near the pool, Frankie the security guard shouted, "Devin? Did you get Mrs. Rychner? I think I see them over by the south entrance!"

Granny Kitty swiped her key card, yanked the door open, and shoved everyone inside. "Let's get up to our suite before we start discussing right, wrong, and who may or may not have stolen rare blue roses that will make Millie Snyder absolutely green with envy when she sees them in our garden."

With everyone inside, Granny Kitty yanked the door shut again, securing the lock. Then they all booked it up the stairs to the top floor as fast as two thirteen-year-olds, two seventy-year-olds, and two Seifes could possibly go.

Which was pretty fast when everyone was afraid of being arrested.

Once inside their hotel room, the grannies stuffed the stolen rosebushes into the bathtub. Amelia took out the book she'd found at the dig site before hiding their clown costumes in her suitcase.

(Meanwhile, the two Seifes did some hiding of their own. Mainly themselves in their beds.)

Right as someone knocked on the door.

"Try to look innocent!" Granny Pearl hissed as Granny Kitty hunched over and assumed her sweet-little-old-lady persona.

Perching her glasses on her nose, Granny Kitty opened the door to reveal Jayla Rychner. She wore a pair of black silk pajamas that resembled a suit. Amelia's mother owned an identical pair. The realization made Amelia's insides go all wiggly as she joined Sloane on the couch.

Panicking, she realized she was holding the stolen book. Stuffing it under one of the cushions, Amelia picked up a newspaper and pretended to read it.

While Sloane buried her nose in a game on her phone.

Tall enough to easily look over Granny Kitty's head, Jayla Rychner regarded both Sloane and Amelia with the air of someone who was none-too-happy about being dragged back to work in the middle of the night. Two fog-dampened teenagers in Cedar Point polo shirts stood on either side of her. Frankie and Devin, presumably.

In a faint voice, Granny Kitty quavered, "Oh, hello? Who are you?"

"And why are you waking us up? Is something wrong?" Granny Pearl whimpered. "Oh dear! Where is my cane?"

Granny Kitty hobbled back into the room like she didn't speed-walk at least five miles every day.

Jayla Rychner followed her, clearly not buying it. "Yes, I'm afraid something *is* wrong. My security guards spotted two rather short people breaking into Dr. Jamil's archaeological dig. Before running through a very dangerous construction site."

"It was Maniac McGee! He came back as a ghost clown!" Devin looked very much like he'd seen a ghost. Bug-eyed, slack-jawed, twitchy.

Looking over his shoulder like he expected Maniac McGee to creep up on him at any moment.

Frankie inched away from him.

Jayla Rychner tried to calm him down, using the same soothing voice a parent would use with a toddler scared by a nightmare. "Devin, I think we can all agree that it was a living person who only looked like a ghost clown in the fog." Turning to Sloane and Amelia, she used a very different tone. "What do the two of you know about this supposedly ghostly intruder?"

Sloane and Amelia immediately sat up straighter.

"Nothing!" Amelia squeaked, embarrassment swallowing her freckles.

"I think you should talk to Dr. Pickerington." Sloane managed to sound innocent. However, if Jayla Rychner had known her better, the Cedar Point manager would have noticed that Sloane was nervously wrapping the tip of her ponytail round and round her finger. "She doesn't seem to like Dr. Jamil very much. But she definitely likes costumes."

Jayla Rychner sucked in her breath. She crossed her arms suspiciously.

In her I-wouldn't-hurt-a-fly voice, Granny Pearl said, "Unless you have some sort of proof that they were involved, I think we'd all better get back to sleep."

Amelia yawned and stretched with exaggerated effort. "Yup! I was having the best dream when you woke me up!"

"You were reading a newspaper," the park manager pointed out tartly.

"*Was* I?" Amelia did her best to imitate the grannies' innocent act. "I had no idea. I must have been doing that in my sleep. No kid reads actual newspapers anymore. Even if they *do* read papers, they read them online. I mean, what is this? 1990?"

She laughed nervously, joined by Sloane.

"So glad that's settled!" Granny Kitty ushered Jayla Rychner, Frankie, and the still-twitching Devin out of their room.

As they stepped outside, Jayla's walkie-talkie crackled. A staticky voice said, *"Hey, we've got reports of a couple of elderly people digging up the rosebushes over by the old lighthouse. Anyone know anything about that?"*

Jaw dropping, Jayla Rychner whipped back around. However, before she could say anything, Granny Kitty slammed the door shut and threw the dead bolt. "Good night! Sleep tight! Don't let the bedbugs bite!" Returning to the rest of them, she stretched and yawned more believably than Amelia had. "Whew! I'm beat! I don't know about you, Pearl, but I'm off to bed!"

Granny Pearl followed, leaving Sloane and Amelia alone.

Amelia swung her attention from the grannies' bedroom door to the door Jayla had exited. "How worried do you think we should be?"

"Worried enough to figure out where that time capsule is before we all get arrested," Sloane sighed. She went over to the refrigerator in the suite's kitchen to get out the box of leftover pizza. "Hey, we never did find out what took my grannies so long in Sandusky."

"Probably digging up the courthouse flower beds." Amelia joined Sloane at the counter. She found a slice of tomato-and-olive pizza, while Sloane attacked the bacon-and-banana-pepper slices. While they ate their snack, Amelia retrieved the book she'd hidden under the couch cushion.

"Whoever broke into Dr. Jamil's office stole this," she explained. "It fell into the hole with us when they were running away."

The book was quite old. With a faded cloth cover gone thread-bare around the edges so that the cardboard underneath could poke through. When Sloane flipped it open after carefully wiping her fingers on a napkin, they discovered the pages inside had come unstuck from the binding. The pages had gone orange with age and were so dry that they crumbled slightly to the touch.

"Rumors and Rewards—The Hidden History of the Founding of Sandusky County," Sloane read.

"I thought Dr. Jamil was interested in the history of Cedar Point *after* the 1800s," Amelia said around a mouthful of cold moz-zarella. "Why would he need this book?"

That was an excellent question.

Together, they flipped through the pages, trying to find the answer.

They quickly found something else instead:

> **Colonel Pike Pickerington, one of Sandusky's early leaders, arrived on the Cedar Point peninsula shortly after the end of the Civil War. Once here, he opened up Pickerington's Cedar Wardrobes. His factory quickly became well-known through-out the United States for his luxury outhouses. The fragrant smell of the cedar wood helped cover up other, less-pleasant odors.**

Sloane spit-laughed at that.

"Dr. Pickerington made such a big deal about how her what-ever-many-great-grandpa made his fortune by selling cedar ward-robes," she snorted, clapping a hand over her mouth to keep her pizza from escaping. "Turns out, he made his fortune in early porta-potties!"

Amelia giggled too—and then stopped as she had a realization.

"Oh! So, Colonel Pike Pickerington owned the outhouse factory in between the coffin factory and Zistel's bathhouses." Amelia pulled up the picture of the old map and showed it to Sloane. "When she was yelling at us earlier today, Dr. Pickerington said that he was good friends with Covington Collymore."

"I can believe that," Sloane said, continuing to flip through the book. "I mean, it sounds like they both got rich doing stuff that other rich people would think was pretty cringe. Then, once they got rich, they tried to cover it up and told their families that they made their money in less-cringey ways."

"Not that everyone forgot, though. Look." Setting down her phone, Amelia pointed to the page to which Sloane had just turned.

> Many of today's members of Sandusky society still turn their noses up at the Collymore Family. Youngsters might only know them from Collymore Automotives and dream of buying a roadster from the shop. However, their parents are less trusting of the family. Those of us who have been around for a few years remember the rumors that Covington Collymore smuggled more than just bodies out of the Sandusky County Jail in his coffins back in the 1860s and '70s. More than one living prisoner went missing after he'd been there. What

was in those cedar boxes he ferried back and forth across the bay, no one can say. But many of those prisoners were spotted on trains out of town. Who knows how many people escaped justice because of Covington Collymore?

"Oh, so *that's* how he did it," Amelia realized. "I know that prisons were pretty gross back then. I mean, everything was pretty gross back then, but especially prisons. People died of all sorts of stuff, so it wouldn't be that strange for a prison to need coffins to ship the bodies back to their families. Covington Collymore would just bring in one more than he needed."

Sloane nodded, following along. "Then the escaping prisoner climbed inside the spare coffin. Out they'd go, back across the water. Covington Collymore would open up the coffin with the extra person and get paid. Then, after he dropped them off, he'd take anything valuable off the dead people."

"All while charging their families for the coffins, too," Amelia concluded, oddly cheery for someone who had just discovered such a grisly tale. "Covington Collymore the Sixth might not like this, but our YouTube subscribers are going to *love* it!"

Someone who might not love what they had discovered was Dr. Pickerington.

For starters, it was clear that she didn't want anyone to say anything bad about Colonel Pike Pickerington. Sloane and Amelia both bet that she was horrified of how he'd really made his fortune and was determined to cover it up.

Could she be the "ghost" who broke into Dr. Jamil's office?

If so, had she stolen *Rumors and Rewards—The Hidden History of the Founding of Sandusky County* because it had embarrassing information on Colonel Pike Pickerington?

Or...

...was it because it included hints about Covington Collymore I?

Because, when she yelled at Sloane and Amelia earlier in the day, Dr. Pickerington had mentioned something about Covington Collymore I. She'd said that he and Colonel Pike Pickerington had been good friends.

Good enough friends for Covington Collymore I to tell Colonel Pike Pickerington about his time capsule?

As well as what was in it?

If so, that seemed to support the theory that there wasn't a boring land deed hidden inside it.

Instead, there could be stolen money and jewelry.

Being a professor probably didn't pay all that much.

Was Dr. Pickerington trying to find the time capsule too?

While they were at it, Sloane pointed out that Jayla Rychner had gotten to Cedar Point with astonishing speed. No more than ten minutes could have passed between when Devin grabbed them at the dig and when the park manager knocked on their hotel door. No one lived close enough to the park to be awoken in the middle of the night, drive across the peninsula, and get to the Breakers Hotel in that time.

Which meant that Jayla Rychner had already been at the park.

Yet dressed in pajamas to make it seem like she'd been at home.

Why the disguise?

Why the lie?

Amelia didn't have an answer to that as they tidied up the kitchen, wiping their crumbs into the trash can and scrubbing pizza grease off the counter. Normally, Amelia wouldn't have thought to do any of that, partly because the Miller-Poes had a cleaning person who came in every day. And partly because anytime she *did* try to help out, everyone in her family always told her she was cleaning things wrong and then "fixed" her mistakes.

However, Sloane had long ago gotten used to helping her single dad with household chores. Besides, in her family, there was no "right" or "wrong" way to do things. Just people helping other people out.

"What about Dr. Jamil?" Amelia suggested as they finished up.

"What about him?" Sloane asked in confusion.

"Can we rule out the possibility that he could be sabotaging his own dig? If there's something valuable in that time capsule, he wouldn't want his students to find it first, would he? So . . . maybe he's causing problems to make sure they don't find it before he does. Maybe that's why maps and books are disappearing."

There were too many possible suspects.

And Sloane and Amelia still had no idea where the time capsule could be buried.

Plus, they had another problem to deal with. When Sloane opened the door to one of the suite's two bathrooms, a pair of blue rosebushes peered out at her from the bathtub.

Like they were kids taking a bath, waiting for her to bring them rubber duckies.

Sloane groaned, causing Amelia to look too.

Amelia pulled the door shut again and pushed her friend

toward the other bathroom. "I don't see anything. Do you see anything?"

"Nope. Nothing," Sloane agreed. She used the bathroom, brushed her teeth, and went to sleep.

However, once Amelia heard her friend snoring in bed next to her (with the Seife kids snoring in the other), Amelia got up. Grabbing a shovel and one of the rosebushes, she carried it downstairs and returned it to the garden outside the closest exit door. That wasn't where the rosebush had come from, of course, but Amelia figured one garden was the same as another to a plant.

Once she'd returned one rosebush to the soil, she did the same with the other.

Then—and only then—did Amelia go to sleep.

Sloane was the first person in her entire life who had ever made Amelia feel like she was good at anything. Which was ridiculous, because Amelia was slowly realizing that she was good at a lot of things.

Including protecting the people she cared about.

Which included Granny Kitty and Granny Pearl.

Even if they were a pair of flower-garden-and-bingo-game obsessed weirdos.

After all, weirdos were Amelia's kind of people.

Thirteen

Bad Reputations

After all the excitement of the night, it might seem safe to assume that Sloane and Amelia had difficulty sleeping. True, the grannies had sorted out Jayla Rychner, but there were still the possibilities of various ghosts to worry about.

However, sometimes you just reach a point where you're so tired that you can't worry about the things that scare you anymore.

Not even ghost clowns or ghost dolls.

However, in the morning, a chilly Amelia woke up to realize she was half-hanging off the bed, with her arm dangling down to the floor. When she tried to wiggle backward, she thumped into something smaller than Sloane. Who should have been the only other person in bed with Amelia.

Instead, *something* had pulled most of the blankets off her and rolled itself up in them.

The haunted Kewpie doll!

Amelia had known it—*she had known it!* Sloane had dismissed her concerns, but—oh.

Oh . . .

The something rolled over and blinked up at her with big—but definitely neither haunted nor doll-like—eyes from under a mound of messy hair and a purple bow.

Skye Seife.

"What are you doing here?" Amelia asked. Followed up with, "Can I have some blankets? I'm so cold."

"Sure." The preschooler unwrapped herself and shoved the comforter in Amelia's direction. "Brighton thought it would be a good idea to sleep with you guys. You know, in case Maniac McGee got the other ghosts together and they all attacked our room."

As she wrapped the comforter around her shivering arms, Amelia looked across Skye at the rest of the bed. Brighton was wedged between his sister and the blissfully snoring Sloane on the other. Because Sloane had brought her own pillow and blankets, she was still happily curled up in her own nest.

Brighton, meanwhile, wore a plastic football helmet and had his arms wrapped around a baseball bat.

Cordelia the concrete goose sat on the floor at the foot of the bed like a guard dog.

Someone had scrawled a ferocious sneer on her face with Granny Pearl's lipstick.

"I did that!" Skye declared proudly. "I told Brighton that Bertram Cordelia will scare off any ghosts that try to attack him in his sleep."

Amelia scratched at her curls and tried to decide if this was better or worse than waking up at home, surrounded by a bossy family.

Just as she decided that it was its own type of weird, a yelp of distress echoed through the hotel suite. Sloane sat bolt upright in bed.

Then rolled out of the way as Brighton woke up, swinging his baseball bat and screaming, "Go away, Maniac!"

Sloane managed to wrench the bat out of his hands as Amelia explained, "If there are any ghosts in here, they're out in the main room."

Actually, the cry had come from the bathroom. As they all discovered when they padded into the living room to see what was going on.

Granny Kitty and Granny Pearl stood in the bathroom doorway. Hands on hips, lips puckered, and scowls creasing their faces.

"Our rosebushes are gone," Granny Kitty observed sourly.

Granny Pearl narrowed her eyes at Sloane. "Sloane-y, do you know anything about this?"

Sloane could honestly say she didn't. Amelia clasped her hands together in a saintly fashion and said, "I guess they just liked it better outside." Then she went into her own bathroom to take a shower and get dressed for the day in a long, green dress, with gloves again, and a hat heaped high with flowers and trailing a long, satin ribbon behind.

By the time she came out, everyone else had gotten dressed and was ready to go downstairs to the hotel restaurant for breakfast. The grannies had gotten over their annoyance that their stolen plants had been un-stolen.

Probably because they already had plans to re-steal them.

Both Sloane and Amelia agreed that they needed to check the station wagon before they left Cedar Point. If they found any plants inside, Sloane would distract Granny Kitty and Granny Pearl while Amelia returned them to the closest patch of soil she could find.

They took the elevator downstairs and got a table on the opposite side of the restaurant from the crowd of silver-and-black We

Dance Better Than U dancers. The grannies got scrambled eggs, whole-wheat toast, and fruit on the side. Sloane and Brighton both ordered omelets and hash browns with pancakes on the side. Skye waited to hear what Amelia ordered, and then insisted on Belgium waffles with extra whipped cream and strawberries, just like her idol. She tried to order them for Bertram Cordelia as well, but Amelia managed to convince the little girl that they'd just upset the goose's concrete stomach.

For once, Brighton wasn't staring at his tablet. And he actually talked to Sloane.

Watching the grannies as they helped Skye heave Bertram Cordelia up into a chair, he said, "You're pretty lucky. Your family is amazing. I wish they were my family."

"Oh." Sloane hadn't expected him to say that. The way he acted, she wasn't at all sure that he wanted his mom to marry her dad. "Well, they might be. Your mom and my dad might get married."

"They might," Brighton agreed pensively. "Or they might not."

With that, he pulled out his tablet.

And dove back into his Pokémon game.

Sloane twisted her ponytail anxiously around her fingertip, trying to decide if she should say something nice to Brighton. Or tell him that he should stop sulking because *she* had it way worse than him since both of his parents were alive even if they weren't living together.

Maybe there was a way to do both?

Fortunately, Granny Kitty and Granny Pearl distracted her by sharing what they'd learned at the Sandusky County Courthouse the day before. Taking out her phone, Granny Kitty explained,

"Granny Pearl had to flirt with a very sweet court clerk to get him to keep the courthouse open so we could go through the records."

"I seduced him so well that he insisted on taking us out to dinner," Granny Pearl added smugly. "Then there was dancing afterward, of course, followed by a late-night bingo game. That's why we were so late."

Impressed, Amelia rested her chin on one gloved fist. She had never once in her life sweet-talked or flirted her way into convincing anyone of anything. And she was pretty certain she never would.

Used to her grannies, Sloane was slightly less impressed. Setting aside her problems with Brighton, she said, "Granny Pearl, you didn't scam that poor man out of money at the bingo game, did you?"

Granny Pearl suddenly became very interested in adding cream and sugar to her cup of coffee. Granny Kitty swiftly stepped in, waving a hand dismissively. "Nonsense! Pearl gave him the best evening he's had in years! That's well worth—er—a few hundred dollars for a steak dinner and losing at bingo."

Sloane opened her mouth to protest, but Granny Kitty hurried on.

"Anyhow! While Pearl was entertaining Hernando, I went through all the land deeds from the 1860s, 1870s, and 1880s. It was dreadfully boring, but I did find something very interesting. Or maybe it's better to say that I *didn't* find anything very interesting, which is what made it interesting."

"Uh, Granny Kitty," Sloane said as respectfully as she could, "have you had enough coffee yet this morning? Or maybe you've had too much? You're not making much sense."

Once again, Granny Kitty waved her hand dismissively. She picked up her coffee and sipped it as though to prove that she was drinking exactly the right amount. "I'm making perfect sense! You see, the Sandusky County Courthouse has kept excellent records of all the land sales in the county from the 1860s to the present day. Every single one of them was there. All except for the land sales on the Cedar Point peninsula. *All* those were missing."

Sloane and Amelia gasped as Granny Kitty smugly set her coffee cup back in its saucer.

"Someone stole them!" Sloane exclaimed as their breakfast arrived.

"But who?" Amelia wondered.

"And what," Granny Kitty finished, "was in them to make those papers worth stealing?"

A clue to the location to the time capsule *had* to be hidden in one of them. It had to be.

But who had taken it? Jayla Rychner, Dr. Jamil, or Dr. Pickerington?

And was it because the time capsule held a deed proving that Covington Collymore VI was owed millions of dollars?

Or was it because it held hundreds of thousands of dollars in stolen cash and jewelry?

The YouTube video Amelia had posted last night was doing well. It had already gotten over twenty thousand views and their subscriber base was climbing. Some of the comments were pretty mean—and at least some of them were obviously members of Mackenzie and CeeCee's dance team.

However, lots of the comments were super supportive.

Mac and CeeCee must have noticed that, too.

Because they kept throwing snotty glances in the direction of Sloane and Amelia.

Who waved cheerfully back at them. Followed by Skye and Bertram Cordelia blowing kisses.

Scowling, Mac and CeeCee stopped after that.

Their breakfast came and they all scarfed it down. The grannies decided to take the Seife kids to the Cedar Point Shores water park for the day. The four of them went upstairs to their rooms to change into swimsuits. Amelia made sure she had her selfie stick, and then she and Sloane headed over to the gate into the main amusement park.

However, when they presented their plastic platinum pass cards at the turnstile, the teenager working it immediately turned serious.

He compared their pictures on his tablet to the real, live Sloane and Amelia several times. Then turned and called over his shoulder, "Hey, Bree! It's those two kids Mrs. Rychner warned us about!"

"What?" Amelia gasped as Sloane went rigid with shock. "What do you mean she 'warned' you about us? What's there to warn about us?"

Actually, both Sloane and Amelia could think of several things.

Apparently, Jayla Rychner had thought about those things too. Because Bree brought over two burly college kids in tight Cedar Point polo shirts and khaki shorts.

"Are you Sloane and Amelia?" Bree asked perkily. She was a girl with bronze skin and dimples and a too-nice demeanor that reminded Sloane of Mackenzie right before she did something particularly evil.

"Uh, yeah?" Sloane swallowed hard as Amelia squeezed the handle of her parasol in terror.

"This is Nate and Natasha! Aren't their names adorable? They're going to escort you around the park!" Bree beamed at Sloane and Amelia like this was the best thing ever. "Everywhere you go, they're going to go. Kind of like your own, personal security team! Isn't that fun?"

Natasha's muscles bulged under her pale skin, and she cracked her knuckles like she spent her free time twisting people into the shape of pretzels for fun. Nate had straight hair and tawny skin and gave the impression of squashing troublemakers into the shape of pancakes with one blow of his fist.

Sloane and Amelia shrank backward.

"Yeah . . . fun . . . ," Sloane agreed.

"So much fun." In fact, so much fun that Amelia suddenly felt several inches shorter than she had been only a few seconds before.

Nate and Natasha both crossed their arms, faces stony.

Behind Sloane and Amelia, someone let out a witchlike cackle.

The girls turned around to watch Mackenzie and CeeCee flounce their way up to the turnstiles in their black-and-silver athletic suits.

"Oh dear," Mackenzie sneered. "Did Jayla Rychner find out about your little midnight adventure?"

CeeCee brayed a laugh, and they sashayed into the park.

"Wait, how did *they* know about that?" Sloane whispered, sticking her head under Amelia's parasol to keep Nate and Natasha from hearing as they entered the park too. "Did Mrs. Rychner tell them? Why would she do that?"

"Forget about that," Amelia hissed back. She jerked her thumb backward, toward Nate and Natasha on the other side of the parasol's dome. "What are we going to do about those two?"

That was an excellent question. One to which neither girl had a good answer. Because Bree had been quite serious. Nate and Natasha followed them everywhere. Silent. Grim-faced. Just waiting for them to do something so the two guards could pick them up and chuck them out of the park.

The plan had been to go over to the archaeology dig, pretend to find the *Rumors* book in the bushes, and return it to Dr. Jamil and his crew. Then, they'd pump everyone for as much information as they could get.

Still hoping to do just that, Sloane and Amelia walked past all the carnival games and fried-food stands. When they reached the archaeological dig and construction site, things at the Master of Mayhem seemed to be going a bit better than yesterday. Wearing a yellow hard hat and the same suit she had the day before, Jayla Rychner watched as another roller-coaster car was sent up the half-built hill. It reached practically the top—almost to the end of what had been built—before it started to shake.

The man working the lever brought the car back down again.

Jayla Rychner and several other people in hard hats bent over a set of blueprints.

At least they weren't yelling at each other today.

Things might be improving for the park manager, but they were going the opposite direction for Osburn and Miller-Poe Investigations. Sloane and Amelia would never be able to do anything with Nate and Natasha watching their every move. Like both guards had microscopes glued to their eyes. Amelia tried to cause a distraction when they got near to the dig, but when Natasha looked away, Nate didn't. And when she got Nate to look away, Natasha didn't.

They simply couldn't pretend to "find" the book since at least one of the guards would realize Sloane already had the book on her.

So, they walked around the gardens in front of the Coliseum and the Pagoda Gift Shop, keeping the archaeological dig in sight the entire time, trying to stall and come up with a plan.

Only, that didn't work either. Because after they'd circled the garden twice, Nate demanded menacingly, "What are you doing? Casing the place?"

Natasha cracked her knuckles again. "Are you planning on robbing the gift shop?"

"No, no!" Amelia hurriedly assured them both.

Nate reluctantly put away the walkie-talkie he'd just raised to his mouth.

Once again, Sloane ducked under Amelia's parasol so she could have a private word with her friend. "Let's ride some rides, okay? Maybe that will throw off their suspicions."

"But I hate rides!" Amelia protested.

"Then why did you come to Cedar Point?" Natasha demanded, shoving her head under the parasol too.

Nate followed her, asking again, "Is it because you're planning on robbing it?"

"No!" Amelia staggered backward to get away from all the faces suddenly invading her space. Looking desperately from the guards to her friend, she panicked. "No! I mean . . . I hate the little kid rides around here. Why don't we ... go ride a roller coaster, Sloane?"

As soon as she said it, Amelia clapped her hands to her mouth.

Why had she said that?

Nate and Natasha looked at her strangely.

Lowering her hands, Amelia managed to say, "I ... covered my mouth to keep in the ... excitement."

And the vomit.

Oh dear.

So. Much. Vomit.

Already churning in her stomach.

Trying to help her friend, Sloane cast about for a solution. What was the easiest roller coaster she could think of? "Hey, let's go over to the Woodstock Express!"

Nate raised a skeptical eyebrow. "Isn't that a kiddie roller coaster?"

"It's for my inner child." Amelia gasped. She tried very hard not to dig her heels into the asphalt path as Sloane dragged her toward the little roller coaster.

No, not toward a little roller coaster.

Toward her doom.

"Sloane, I don't think I can do this," Amelia whispered, horrified to discover there was no line. Why was there no waiting? All the other rides had at least an hour's wait! Some of them, two or three hours.

"Sure, you can," Sloane whispered back encouragingly as they climbed into one of the cars. "It's just like going for a ride in a car, okay? Sometimes there are hills when you ride in a car, right? And your stomach does a little flip-flop? This is just like that."

"I get car sick when that happens!" The ride technician clipped Amelia's harness in place.

Nate and Natasha got into the car behind them, snapping on their own harnesses.

The ride technician returned to the booth and pushed the lever to start the ride . . .

. . . the cart lurched forward . . .

. . . and Amelia shot out of her harness, out of the ride, and back onto the platform.

"Hey! That's super dangerous!" the ride technician cried in horror, throwing the emergency break. Sloane was thrown forward, with only her harness keeping her from being flung out of the ride. Since her car was still next to the platform, she pressed the release button on her straps and jumped out of it too.

"Stop! Didn't you hear what I said about dangerous?" The ride technician tried to grab her. However, the second Sloane got out, Nate and Natasha did too. All three of them ran after Amelia, leaving the ride technician in hysterics as the other riders began to panic, convinced something terrible had happened.

As far as Amelia was concerned, something terrible *had* happened.

At least, that was what her feet seemed convinced of. No matter how hard her brain tried to get them to stop, they just wouldn't.

Not until she'd fled all the way back to the gate by the Breakers Hotel.

Where she collapsed in a sweaty, queasy pile on a park bench.

When a panting Sloane, Nate, and Natasha finally caught up with her, Amelia looked up at them miserably.

"It's not that I don't like roller coasters," she lied. "I just remembered that I needed to upload our next YouTube video."

Nate and Natasha unceremoniously led them through the turnstiles and dumped them outside the park.

Before they left, however, Nate said, "Could we get a picture of you guys before you go? We're actually really big fans of your YouTube channel."

Natasha nodded. "It's super cool that the official BuzzFeed account commented on your last TikTok."

"Wait? What?" Sloane asked, dazed as both of the guards held up their phones to take selfies with her and Amelia.

Amelia managed an equally dazed smile for the picture. Then snatched out her own phone. With her nose practically pressed against the screen, she cried, "They're right! The official BuzzFeed account posted a comment! It's on the video last night and just says—and just says—"

"What does it say?" Sloane grabbed the tip of her ponytail, practically ripping it off her head in anxiety.

"It says . . . 'Totally bingeable.'" Amelia lifted her face up from her phone, eyes huge. Then, her legs did their own thing once more, collapsing and tipping her onto the ground.

"Totally bingeable." Sloane joined her on the cement sidewalk. "BuzzFeed thinks we're . . . totally bingeable?"

Recovering from her shock, Amelia turned practical. "At least the person who runs their social media accounts thinks we are."

"That's still someone at BuzzFeed." Sloane refused to be discouraged.

"That's still someone at BuzzFeed," Amelia agreed.

As Nate and Natasha headed back into the park, Sloane and Amelia remained sitting on the sidewalk. The other park visitors streamed around them. Amelia checked her other accounts. "Sloane, we have over two hundred thousand subscribers to our YouTube channel now."

Sloane pulled up their other accounts. "We have even more than that on TikTok. And almost as many on Instagram."

The two of them gazed at each other in wonder. Then, the dreamy smile on Sloane's face cracked apart. "That's over two hundred thousand people expecting new content."

Amelia's own smile wavered and then slid away. "And we still have no real idea where Collymore hid his time capsule."

"Let alone what's inside."

"And now over two hundred thousand people *and* BuzzFeed are watching to see what we find out."

With a grimace, they both looked back at the park entrance. Dimpled Bree stood at the gate, watching them. She gave them a friendly little finger wave.

Sloane and Amelia waved back at her.

But they knew what that friendly little finger wave really meant.

Step back inside, and I'll have Nate and Natasha twist you into pretzels.

Pretzels with whom Nate and Natasha would want to take pictures.

But pretzels all the same.

If they were going to get back inside, they needed two things.

Disguises.

And a distraction.

An hour later, the grannies and the Seife kids approached a different gate. This one went from the water park into the amusement park. They dragged the wagon behind them, and right after they went through the turnstiles, something terrible happened. Bertram Cordelia wobbled out of the wagon bed and into the soft dirt of a decorative garden. While the goose managed to avoid chipping her concrete beak, Skye immediately turned hysterical.

Throwing herself down on the ground next to the fallen lawn ornament, she shrieked, "SHE'S DEAD! SHE'S DEAD!"

There's nothing quite like shouting that someone's dead to get the attention of everyone around. The guards in the booth ran over, as did the teenagers monitoring the turnstiles.

As did every park guest around.

With no one watching them, Sloane and Amelia stepped forward and swiped their platinum passes. Their pictures immediately appeared on an abandoned tablet, red lights flashing a warning around the border.

But since there was no one there to see it, they continued on into the park.

Completely unnoticed.

Of course, eventually, someone would notice their pictures and the flashing red light. However, Sloane and Amelia had planned for that as well. Amelia had ditched the long, flowy Victorian gowns and gloves. Instead, she wore a perfectly ordinary pair of shorts and a tank top. Her bushy red hair mostly stuffed under a baseball cap. Sloane likewise wore sunglasses and a most un-Sloane-like sundress. Her long, black hair fell loose around her shoulders rather than being twisted into its usual ponytail.

Neither one of them looked even a little bit like themselves.

Which was the point, of course.

Once Bree or Jayla Rychner or anyone realized that Sloane and Amelia were in the park, they'd have all the employees searching.

Searching for two kids who looked nothing like what Sloane and Amelia now looked.

To complete the look, they played a couple of games, winning a squid hat for Sloane to wear and a stuffed Minion for Amelia to carry around.

No one bothered them as they sauntered over to the archaeological dig. Trent, Clara, AJ, and Ryan were all hard at work beneath the sun-blocking tent. Using brushes to wipe away fine dirt, and small pick axes to tap objects free from the hard-packed clay.

Amelia pretended to spot the threadbare *Rumors* book in the bushes.

"Hey. Yo. Whaddya think about dis?" Amelia said in a very exaggerated accent, waving the book about.

"What sort of accent is that?" Sloane stared at her friend in confusion.

"A New York accent!" Amelia beamed proudly. "You know, to go along with our disguises."

The college kids climbed out of the dig to come over and see what had been "found."

Clara pulled off a dirty pair of work gloves so she could take the book from Amelia. "Oh hey, Amelia. What's up with the accent?"

Amelia's shoulders slumped. "You recognize us?"

"Not from a distance," Trent explained. "But why wouldn't we recognize you once we got closer?"

"No reason," Amelia sighed in disappointment.

Clara, however, quickly distracted her. "I think this is one of Dr. Jamil's books."

"His office was broken into again last night." Ryan put his hands on his hips to glare at the two middle schoolers like he suspected the two of them.

Sloane and Amelia made an effort to look as saintly as possible.

"NO! You don't say?" Amelia gasped. She was very good at filming and editing their YouTube videos, but she wasn't a very good actress.

More convincing of the two of them, Sloane raised her eyebrows. "Really?"

"Yeah, the ghost of Maniac McGee returned," Trent said earnestly. "Totally scared my friend, Devin, who was working guard duty last night."

"No way that was a ghost." AJ shook his head. "The burglar stepped on a Kewpie doll and broke it into about twenty different pieces. Now I have to glue it all back together again."

Hastily, Sloane moved them away from the topic of who might or might not have broken the Kewpie doll. She offered to buy them all some frozen custard. Even with the tent to block the scorching sunlight, all four of them dripped with sweat. Ryan refused and snootily swiped the book to take back to Dr. Jamil's office.

Everyone else gratefully accepted the offer. They settled with their cones in the grassy shade of a cedar tree that was so big, it must have been there when Collymore I was running around, digging up Cedar Point and burying his time capsule.

"Why would Dr. Jamil need that book anyhow?" Amelia asked as they all slurped their treats. "I mean, you guys are mainly interested in objects from the early nineteen hundreds, right? That book was all about gossip from before then."

Trent shrugged. "I dunno. I think he just likes knowing about stuff from the eighteen hundreds so he can annoy Dr. Pickerington."

He stopped talking then as his ice cream had started to run down his fingers. As Trent focused on keeping his cone from collapsing, AJ picked up. "Honestly, we all think that the only reason Dr. J hasn't returned that book to the library is to drive her crazy."

Clara nodded. "Apparently, she called the Sandusky Library, trying to get them to get it back from Dr. Jamil. See, he's got it on long-term loan and doesn't have to give it back until the end of the summer. For some reason, she really doesn't want him to have it."

Sloane and Amelia had a pretty good idea what that reason was.

Well, two possible reasons, actually.

One was Pickerington's Porta-Potties—or whatever they'd been called.

Two, she was looking for the buried time capsule.

The real question was, was Dr. Jamil looking for it too? Most of their followers were younger than him, but if anyone his age was going to be a fan of a historical cold case YouTube series, it was probably going to be someone like him.

"You don't suppose he could be trying to find anything from the 1800s, do you?" Sloane asked carefully, trying not to make it seem like a big deal.

Clara scrunched her face in confusion. "Like what?"

"Like . . . I dunno. Something valuable?" Sloane waved her own ice-cream cone around like the idea had just occurred to her.

All three of the college students looked at each other.

Then burst out laughing.

"I think you've watched too many movies," Trent said. "Archaeologists don't look for buried treasure. That's just made up."

As the archaeology students thanked them for the treat and returned to their dig, Amelia's phone binged.

It was Covington Collymore VI.

And he wanted to meet up with them.

To hear about everything they'd discovered so far.

Which . . . wasn't anything he was going to like.

Fourteen

Like any good amusement park—or even any bad amusement park—Cedar Point has a Ferris wheel.

This one looms over the eastern side of the park and stands 145 feet in the air. This makes it as tall as a twelve-story sky scraper. Behind it, a thin band of beach stretches along the aqua-blue waters of Lake Erie. At the very top of the Ferris wheel, riders can see for miles across the lake, as well as all across the amusement park.

At night, its spokes glowed different colors.

It's a terrific Ferris wheel to ride ... if you like Ferris wheels.

If you don't, then it's a terrible Ferris wheel to ride.

And an even worse one if you have to ride it while giving someone bad news.

"Nope. Uh-uh. No way." Amelia took one look and parked herself on the nearest bench and wrapped her ankles around its wrought iron legs. Then she twisted her elbows around the armrests, like she thought Sloane might try to pry her off it.

No one could have paid Sloane enough to do that. Not only did she not want to force her friend to do something Amelia clearly didn't want to do. She'd seen what spewed out of Amelia when people tried it.

Holding up her hands, Sloane backed away. "Why don't I handle this meeting? I'll say you're following up on some clues, okay?"

"Okay," Amelia agreed unhappily, very annoyed with herself. She didn't want to make Sloane go without her. It made Amelia feel like a wimp, letting down her fellow detective. How could they be Osburn and Miller-Poe Investigations if only Osburn did the investigating?

Why couldn't she be brave like Sloane?

Sloane faced her fears, no matter how wobbly legged she might be.

She didn't sit on benches, ignoring a FaceTime call coming through from her family.

As Amelia did that, Sloane walked over to the line for the Ferris wheel. Covington Collymore waved at her from over by the Fast Pass line. CeeCee and Mackenzie stood with him, both with arms crossed sulkily.

"Hey, Sloane!" Covington Collymore grinned at her. He looked very dad-at-an-amusement park in a T-shirt, khakis, and baseball cap. Effortlessly expensive T-shirt, khakis, and baseball cap. "Where's Amelia?"

"Probably off being a loser," CeeCee giggled. Mackenzie barked out a laugh like it was the funniest thing she'd ever heard.

Sloane stared coldly back at Mac, while Covington Collymore told his daughter, "Aw, come on, CeeCee. Different people are into different things."

He turned away to check in their passes.

"*Loser* things," Mackenzie snickered, keeping her voice low enough that Collymore couldn't hear her, but Sloane could.

"Please post that on TikTok." Sloane kept her chin high. "Since you began posting about us, we've practically quadrupled our followers on YouTube."

Both girls' smug faces flattened into scowls.

Sloane, however, beamed as the ride attendant led them to their carriage.

"Have you already ridden the Ferris wheel this morning?" the attendant asked Sloane.

"No, why?"

"You just look sort of familiar, that's all. I'd swear I've seen you somewhere." Scratching his head, he returned to his station.

Sloane slunk down as far in her seat as she could.

She was pretty sure she only looked familiar because Jayla Rychner had shared hers and Amelia's photographs with all the workers.

Probably with the warning to call security, if they were spotted.

CeeCee and Mackenzie sat on one side of the carriage and busied themselves taking selfies and looking out the opening at the lake beyond. While Sloane and Collymore VI sat on the other side to discuss the case. As the wheel arced slowly upward, the amusement park dropped away. Growing smaller and smaller until it looked like a toy model of a park with little figurines moving around rather than real people.

The lake grew and grew, the higher up they went, the blue of the waves merging together with the blue of the sky.

Until it felt like the boats zipping across the water could fly right up into the sky.

Sails becoming kites.

Kites flowing downward to become sails, gliding across the lake to Canada.

Just like Maniac McGee had tried to do.

Tried—and failed—with the help of Collymore's ancestor.

"And 'the great ships sail outward and return, bending and bowing o'er the billowy swells,'" Collymore said, slinging his elbow over the back of the seat so he could look outward.

"What's that?" Sloane asked, startled out of her own thoughts.

"The line from my great-great-great-grandfather's letter," Collymore reminded her, still staring out at the water from behind his sunglasses. "He loved this lake and this land. Zistel took that from him, and I want to right that wrong. Have you found out where the time capsule is hidden yet?"

"Well, um." Sloane wished that Amelia was here. The other girl was much better at making things sound fancier and more important than they really were.

Plus, she could tell that CeeCee and Mackenzie were secretly recording her.

Anything she said was likely to find its way online.

Needing time to think, Sloane took her own phone out of her pocket and pulled up the picture she'd taken of the letter Collymore I had written to his wife a hundred years before. "So, we've managed to confirm that the archaeological dig hasn't found anything yet. Though lots of people are acting kind of suspicious around it. Therefore we, uh, can't rule out that they might be looking for it too."

"Yes, yes." Collymore waved his hand impatiently. "I already knew that. What new information have you found?"

In spite of the cool lake breeze blowing her hair around under her squid hat, Sloane suddenly found herself sweating.

It did not help that CeeCee and Mackenzie were watching her like two gleeful cats getting ready to gobble up a mouse.

Desperate, she started to read from the source material. "Um, well, your great-great-great-grandfather says, 'I can feel myself sailing off into my final sunset.' So, um, we definitely feel the time capsule is pretty near the shore. Which both the Coliseum and the Pagoda Gift Shop are. So, yeah, those seem the most likely spots. He also mentions that, 'The corner stone on which all lies rest will show itself to be a fake and crumble.' Which . . . Oh!"

As she'd been speaking, Sloane had looked up nervously from her phone. However, she'd been afraid that if she looked Collymore in the eye, he'd know she was stalling. So, instead, she'd swept her gaze across the amusement park.

To where a bulldozer dug at a side of a brick restroom that was being torn down.

Starting with the corner.

The corner*stone*.

A long time ago, Sloane had taken a very boring tour of a very boring mansion in Washington, D.C. with her parents. On the tour, the guide had mentioned that, sometimes, people used to hollow out a building's cornerstone and put things inside to bring good luck to the people who lived there. It was literally the only interesting thing on a long, dull tour during which Sloane had just wanted to visit the gift shop.

She'd forgotten all about it until now.

Mackenzie's snide giggle brought Sloane back to herself.

With a jerk, she realized that everyone else in the carriage was staring at her. In exasperation, Collymore said to her, "You're just telling me things that I already knew. Haven't you found out anything?"

"The cornerstone," Sloane gasped. Then, collecting herself, she continued with more confidence. "We think you're wrong about the time capsule being buried somewhere on the peninsula. Even in 1915, a lot of Cedar Point had been dug up more than once. We think the first Collymore would have realized how risky it would be to bury it. So, we think he hid it in a cornerstone of one of the buildings instead."

Collymore sat up straighter. The laughing, superior sneers dropped from Mackenzie and CeeCee's faces. CeeCee turned off her phone and lowered it.

"Do you have any idea which building?" Collymore asked as the Ferris wheel spun them slowly back toward the ground.

"We're still working on that." Sloane made it sound like they had some ideas. "But I don't want to say too much before we know more."

Or anything at all.

Pleased, Collymore nodded. To his daughter, he said, "See, CeeCee? I told you hiring Osburn and Miller-Poe Investigations was a good idea!"

CeeCee gave Sloane a look that made Sloane glad the carriage had finally returned them to the ground.

Before CeeCee and Mac chucked her out of the carriage and into the water.

Escaping, Sloane ran back to the bench where she'd left Amelia. "Amelia! I've just had an idea! What if the time capsule—"

Sloane didn't finish her sentence.

Nate and Natasha sat on either side of her friend.

They weren't taking selfies, either.

Instead, they looked like two lumps of stone. Capable of crushing troublesome park visitors between them.

A miserable Amelia swept the baseball cap off her head. She crushed it nervously between her fingers as a dimpled Bree stood nearby. "Hi, Sloane! We're *so* excited you decided to return to the park! Isn't this a fun place? And speaking of fun, Mrs. Rychner would really like to see you! Doesn't that sound like even more fun?"

Bree crinkled her nose and squeezed her clipboard against her chest. Like she was having trouble keeping all her happiness inside.

That or the chomped-up remains of all the troublesome park visitors she'd eaten after Nate and Natasha crushed them up for her.

Sloane and Amelia followed Bree back to the offices inside the Convention Center. Jayla Rychner sat at her desk, typing away on her laptop. Looking up, she waved away stony-faced Nate and Natasha, as well as the too-perky Bree. Who gave Sloane and Amelia a little finger wave on the way out. "Byeeeee!"

They returned the wave with less enthusiasm.

Jayla Rychner snapped her laptop shut. She carefully folded her fingers together and rested her chin on them.

Sloane swallowed hard and tried not to fidget.

Amelia hunched her shoulders, feeling the way she did when her mom wasn't happy with her.

When the park manager finally spoke, both girls jumped. "I hear that the two of you discovered a stolen book by the archaeology site. That's quite a miracle."

"It must have been dropped by the thief who broke in last night," Amelia squeaked.

Jayla Rychner arched an eyebrow. "And how did you know about that?"

"Erm, social media?" Sloane suggested as Amelia flamed bright red and tried to shrink farther down into her shoulders.

"We've kept it off social media." Jayla Rychner would have made a great spy interrogator. She had yet to take her eyes off either girl. Sloane wasn't sure she'd even blinked.

In spite of the seriousness of their situation, Amelia couldn't help but snort. "Yeah, right. Try keeping *anything* off social media." Then, seeing the way Jayla was glaring at her, she hastily added, "Other than that, I mean!"

Rolling her eyes, Jayla Rychner sighed and finally unclasped her fingers. She stood up and came around the side of her desk. Sloane and Amelia inched closer to each other, just in case she had something horrible planned for them.

Instead, she said, "I don't believe for a second that the two of you are the cause of all the trouble at the dig. However, after the events of last night, I checked out your social media accounts. I see that Covington Collymore has hired you to look for some sort of time capsule?"

Neither Sloane nor Amelia knew what to say to that. On the one hand, admitting that it was true felt weirdly like admitting to a crime. On the other hand . . . well, it was true. And out there on social media, just like Jayla Rychner had pointed out.

So . . . well . . .

"Yeah," Sloane admitted with a shrug.

With it all out in the open, Amelia grew bolder. "I mean, don't you think it's kind of weird that all the land deeds that show which people owned what are missing from the Sandusky County Courthouse?"

Jayla sighed again and clapped a hand to the side of her head like she was developing quite a headache. She gestured for the two of them to follow her as she went over to a cabinet next to her wall of maps. "They're missing because we got special permission from the county to keep them here years ago. We have a museum all about the history of the park."

Opening up the cabinet, she took out a set of very old documents. Printed on heavy cardstock grown yellow with time. All the fonts were incredibly fancy, as though looking artistic was more important than being easy to read. It seemed to be a nineteenth century version of a standard form. Blanks had been left for people to fill in with equally fancy handwriting.

She held it out for Sloane and Amelia to take. They read:

In the year of our Lord eighteen-hundred-and-seventy-five, I, Covington Collymore, do sign over twenty acres of woodland to Louis Zistel in exchange for the amount of $100.00.

Startled, Sloane looked up at the park manager. "Does

Covington Collymore—you know, the Covington Collymore who's alive right now. Not the dead one—anyhow, does Collymore know about this?"

The park manager waved an exasperated hand. "Of course! He came to me, all upset when he first heard about the archaeological dig. Said we needed to put a stop to it. Then, when I wouldn't, he started in on how his family really owns this land. Which meant that he should have some say in what was and was not dug up. It's all a bunch of nonsense, and he knows it. Yet he just kept insisting that I stop the dig! Between him and Dr. Pickerington—"

"What's that about Dr. Pickerington?" Amelia asked.

Sighing, Jayla Rychner shook her head. "She doesn't like the dig, either. Apparently, she and Dr. Jamil have quite a rivalry or something. At least, that's what I assume it is. She just keeps saying he's trying to ruin history. I'm not quite sure how he could do that."

Both Sloane and Amelia were quite sure that the "history" Dr. Pickerington was worried about was the one she'd made up. The version of history in which her ancestor *didn't* get rich by becoming the nation's leader in outhouse manufacturing.

The bigger question for the two of them was: Why had Covington VI lied to them?

"It has to be because he thinks there's money or jewelry or something inside the time capsule," Amelia said after they'd returned to their hotel suite. She spoke from behind the bathroom door as she changed out of her boring shorts and T-shirt and was back in far more interesting clothing.

"Yeah, but he's rich," Sloane objected from the bedroom where she was changing into more comfortable clothing. "He doesn't need that stuff."

"That we know about. Maybe his business, Collymore Automotives, isn't doing as well as he acts like it is. Besides, rich people always want to get richer."

Sloane and Amelia had the place all to themselves. The grannies and the Seife kids were still at the water park. Apparently, they had their own versions of Nate and Natasha standing guard over them. Since neither Granny Kitty nor Granny Pearl was up to anything (for a change), they were actually pleased about this. Both grannies sent photos of their two, hulking guards fanning them, bringing them tropical drinks . . .

And—eventually—playing old maid with them.

"Oh man," Sloane groaned, furiously texting her grannies a reminder that those college kids probably weren't getting paid very well and needed every penny of their paychecks. Her message sent, she turned her attention to Amelia's explanation of Collymore's behavior. "Yeah, but why lie to us about that?"

"Maybe because we have too many people following us now," Amelia suggested, coming out of the bathroom in another long Victorian dress. "Maybe he didn't want us to include that information and then have someone else find it before us. Especially when Jayla Rychner, Dr. Jamil, and Dr. Pickerington might already be looking for it."

"We'll figure that out later," Sloane said. "Listen to this theory I came up with while I was up on the Ferris wheel with Mr. Collymore. It's about that reference to the cornerstone."

She shared what she'd realized as she watched the bulldozer tear down the brick restrooms.

If Collymore I had somehow managed to hollow out one of the cornerstones, then he could have hidden his time capsule in any building. It wouldn't matter that the land around them had been dug up or changed. The time capsule could still be there.

They could still do it.

They could still find the missing time capsule.

Wow Covington Collymore and BuzzFeed all at once.

And finally make Mackenzie and CeeCee stop laughing at them for good.

Fifteen

The trouble with being banned from a place is that, well . . . you're banned from it.

Meaning you can't go inside.

Which is a problem when you really, really want to be inside.

The area around the Coliseum, the Pagoda Gift Shop, and the Convention Center still seemed like the most likely spots for Covington Collymore I to have hidden his time capsule. All three were close to where his cabinet/coffin shop had been located. Now that they had their first solid lead—Sloane's idea about the cornerstone—they needed to take a shovel and whack at their corners and see if anything interesting fell out.

Sort of like piñatas.

Unfortunately, Sloane and Amelia couldn't figure out how to get back into Cedar Point when it was still daylight.

So, they checked out the hotel instead.

Walking around it with one of the grannies' shovels slung over Sloane's shoulder. Using it to tap all the stones forming each corner of the hotel on the unlikely chance that Collymore I had hollowed out one of these stones, shoved his deed or stolen goods or whatever inside—and then covered it up with mortar.

A hollowed-out stone should sound different than a solid stone.

The trouble of it was, neither Sloane nor Amelia knew what a hollowed-out stone sounded like.

Not even after watching several YouTube videos claiming that it was super easy.

Maybe it was, and they just hadn't found the right stone.

Or maybe it wasn't super easy, and they'd already passed it over, not realizing it.

Sloane put her ear against their latest cornerstone and tapped it with the tip of the shovel.

Clink-clink-clink.

She turned to Amelia. "Did that sound like a hollowed-out stone to you?"

Amelia stopped filming Sloane, as she'd been doing in the hopes of catching it on film when they discovered the lost time capsule. She scrunched up her face thoughtfully and then shrugged. "It didn't sound like any of the videos. They sounded more like clunk-clunk-clunk. Not clink-clink-clink."

Sloane sighed and tried another one.

Making a face, Amelia lifted up her camera again.

They were crouching in the landscaped gardens along one side of the Breakers Hotel. More rosebushes filled it, making their work extra prickly and delicate. Not only did they have to avoid the thorns, Amelia kept getting mulch in her shoes, and Sloane got splinters in her knees.

"Hey, what are you kids doing in there?" demanded a man in a floppy hat and dirt-covered work gloves. He pushed a wheelbarrow filled with even more of the shredded wood chips that made up the mulch.

"Um, gardening?" Amelia said, only to realize that her camera gave her away. "Well, she's gardening, and I'm filming it for our Instagram group's Instagram page. We're part of a community service group? It's called—uh—Girls Who Garden. It's to get more girls into the . . . gardening industry."

Amelia had to force herself not to wince as the words tumbled out of her mouth.

Even to her own ears, the lie didn't exactly sound believable.

Behind her, thinking the same thing, Sloane tensed herself to jump up and run.

Then the gardener rolled his eyes and dumped his wheelbarrow full of mulch at their feet. "Whatever. I need a break anyhow. When you're done here, go take care of the peony bushes, would ya?"

Sloane and Amelia both recoiled in horror at the thought.

However, the gardener didn't notice and quickly got out of there. As the sun slowly sank on the other side of the park, they made their way to every outside corner of the Breakers Hotel.

Nothing.

Or, at least, nothing that they could find.

Hot, sweaty, and disgruntled, they returned the shovel to the grannies' station wagon.

Sloane checked her phone. "We still need to check the Eerie Estate. You know, where that Boeckling guy lived? The one who bought Cedar Point from Zistel? It's not on any of the maps because they only use it during HalloWeekends in the fall. I sent my dad a text, asking him if he remembered where it is. But he hasn't gotten back to me yet. Not that it matters if we can't find a way into the amusement park without Bree setting Nate and

Natasha on us. If they're suspicious of us when we're just walking around, imagine what they'd do if we took a hammer or a shovel to the buildings."

She sat down on the car's fender in defeat.

"Oh!" Amelia's eyes went wide. She clapped a hand into her curls—and then grimaced. "Erf. I have an idea. Ugh. A very, very, *very* bad idea."

"How bad of an idea can it be?" Sloane asked, also straightening up. "We don't have any other ideas."

"It involves my family."

"Oh." Sloane grimaced too. "Erf. Ugh."

"And we'll have to leave the shovel here . . ."

Amelia explained what she was thinking as the two of them walked once more to the back gate. By now, the sun had begun to set, pouring hazy orange light over the park. A purple twilight crept across the lake, with stars and satellites sparkling within it. Exhausted parents dragged wagons toward their cars in the parking lot. Within those wagons, children cried, not wanting the fun to end. Or else flopped facedown in the wagon bed, even more tired than their parents.

Lots wore glow-in-the-dark bands or held light-up souvenirs.

Only one teenage worker remained at the entrance, bored and on his phone. As Sloane and Amelia approached, he didn't even bother to look up. "Sorry, but we're not letting anyone else in. The park is closing in fifteen minutes."

"But I left my parasol inside!" Amelia cried, squeezing her hands together in despair. "Please! It's very important to me! And my parents will be so mad—at anyone who doesn't let me look for it!"

The teenager stared at her, clearly unimpressed.

He turned his attention back to his phone, mumbling again, "The park is closing."

Ugh. Amelia scrunched up her face . . .

. . . and pulled out her own phone and FaceTime-ed her family.

"Um, Mom, Dad—I need your help." At first, the word stuck in Amelia's throat. She had to squeeze them out. After spending most of her thirteen years desperately trying to convince them that she *didn't* need their help, saying those words was worse than puking. *Way* worse. "I've lost my parasol! And this guy won't let me back in the park to look for it!" Amelia swiveled her camera toward the teenager so they could see him. When he looked up, startled, she shoved the camera in his face.

"What is your name, young man?" the Judge bellowed. *"I want your full name right now! No mumblings or excuses! I want your name, and the name of your manager! And the name of your manager's manager! No, the name of the CEO of your company! I'll have you know that I am a very important person, and you do not want to cross me!"*

"But—but—but—" the poor teenager sputtered. Life had not prepared him to deal with the loud, aggressive entitlement of the Miller-Poe Family. Without thinking, he took the phone from Amelia as he tried to defend himself. "I'm just following the rules!"

Amanda Miller thrust her face in view of the camera. *"We're serious! We want to talk to your manager right now! 'Following rules'? HA! You're bullying children, that's what you're doing!"*

The Miller-Poe tirade continued as Sloane and Amelia slunk past the poor kid and into the park. Even in the gathering darkness,

Amelia's embarrassment flamed across her freckled face.

"Do you think he'll be okay? You don't think they'll get him fired, do you?" she asked Sloane as they skimmed the streetlights and slid into the shadows to avoid being spotted.

"I don't think so," Sloane whispered back. She pulled Amelia deeper into the shadows as a cleanup crew passed. Sweeping at the sidewalk with their brooms. After the crew continued on their way, Sloane added, "Though he might need years of therapy."

"Who doesn't?" Amelia sighed.

A loudspeaker announced the end of the day. The roller coasters ground to a halt. The Ferris wheel stopped spinning. The last of the weary revelers staggered out of the gates. Workers pulled shutters down over the carnival games, tucking the stuffed animals inside for the night. Shop doors were locked, and the workers soon followed the guests out the gate.

Still, the cleaning crews remained.

As did the guards.

And they all knew that Sloane and Amelia were still inside.

"Mrs. Rychner has sent photos of these two kids to everyone's phones," Bree explained to a cleaner as Sloane and Amelia hunched under the cover of a nearby bush. "If you spot them, you're to stop them and call her immediately."

"How much trouble can a couple of kids be?" the cleaning person asked, leaning on his broom.

"You have no idea." Bree swung a flashlight suspiciously around the wooded area where the middle schoolers squatted in the mulch.

Her light missed them to Sloane and Amelia's sagging relief.

Satisfied, Bree marched off, but more guards remained. Using flashlights to poke holes in the shadows, feeling about for Sloane and Amelia. Who crawled slowly from tree to tree, then dashed behind restrooms and shuttered concession stands. All while holding their breath out of fear that their panting would give them away if the slap of their sneakers didn't.

"Do you think we've managed to avoid all the security cameras?" Amelia asked as they reached the archaeological dig.

"Let's not worry about that right now," Sloane said. Even though she was, actually, pretty worried about that.

None of the guards seemed to have been looking at the right camera at the right time, so far.

But if Sloane and Amelia found a hollow cornerstone and smashed it open, Jayla Rychner would *definitely* be checking the tapes.

First, however, they had to locate the correct cornerstone and bash their way into it.

To that end, they were going to borrow a few tools from the archaeological dig.

Skirting the edge of the roped off area, they went over to the toolbox and opened the lid. Out of the chest, they took a pointed pickax, a small hammer, and a heavy mallet.

Closing it, they tiptoed over to the edge of the Coliseum. With no guard in sight, they began tapping all the various stones around the corner.

Clunk-clunk-clunk, went the hammer.

Against stone after stone.

They all sounded exactly the same.

Sloane looked at Amelia and shrugged. They moved on to the next corner, and then the next.

None of them sounded any different than the others.

Darting around the little kid rides of cars and planes that spun in circles (when turned on), they moved on to the Convention Center.

Every single stone near the corner sounded exactly like every other stone.

Which was exactly what they got at the Pagoda Gift Shop, too.

"Gah!" Sloane hissed in frustration. She wanted to pound the hammer against the ground. However, not only would that be childish, it would probably catch the attention of one of the guards.

"Ooo! Sloane, your phone just lit up!" Amelia pointed at Sloane's back pocket in excitement. "Is it your dad? Does he remember where the Eerie Estate is?"

The Eerie Estate was where George A. Boeckling had lived after he bought Cedar Point from the people who had bought it from Zistel. Maybe when he'd bought the park, he'd also bought Collymore's weird grudge without realizing it.

Regardless, they needed to check out the mansion since it had been on the peninsula in 1915.

Sloane read the message. "It is—and he does! And it's right over by here—just behind the Convention Center!"

As soon as Sloane said it, a guard was swinging a flashlight around the garden in the main causeway. Even though he was looking the wrong way, he was moving close enough to hear him.

Sloane and Amelia crouched even lower and crawled in

the direction of the mansion. By the time they reached it, their muscles ached—but at least they'd avoided detection. A fine powder of paint and stone dust coated their hands from banging on the stones. Every mosquito on the peninsula seemed to have decided that the two of them were the tastiest things around. Ignoring it all, the two detectives focused on solving their mystery.

Once more, they went around to each of the building's four corners. Tap-tap-tapping as they went.

Once more, they didn't find anything.

"I was so sure I was right!" Frustrated, Sloane slumped onto the ground. In spite of the wind and the cooling night air, sweat soaked the back of her shirt. While mosquito bites made itchy patterns up and down her legs.

"All this for nothing." Amelia sat down next to her, just as miserable. "I've lost my phone—who knows if I'll even be able to get it back? We've got nothing we can use in another video, and if I don't post something tomorrow, all our followers will know it. It'll look like Mackenzie and CeeCee were right, and we really don't know what we're doing. Then, all the people defending us online will stop. BuzzFeed will unfollow us, and everyone will know that people were right not to believe in me—in us. I mean, me. People believe in you for other reasons, like being good at softball. Everyone thinks I'm a loser weirdo, and now they're going to see that they're right."

To Amelia's horror, she felt a tear slide down her nose. She scrubbed at it furiously, but she ended up getting grit in her eyes. Which just made it worse.

Sloane patted her shoulder reassuringly. "Amelia, I think you might be catastrophizing."

"Catastrophizing?" Amelia snuffled.

"You know, when you turn something a little bad into a full catastrophe?"

"Well, it *feels* like a catastrophe." Amelia found a clean spot on her sleeve and used it to clean her eyes.

"Yeah," Sloane sighed. "It feels that way to me right now, too. But you know, we always think of something. If we can escape someone who wanted to knock us out and feed us to the coyotes back on our first case, we'll find a way around this, too."

The sound of footsteps reached their ears. Sloane and Amelia jumped to their feet and pressed themselves back against the shadowy side of the mansion. Instead of a guard's voice, however, a very familiar voice reached them.

"They're over this way, Mrs. Rychner," Mackenzie announced confidently.

What? *What?* Both Sloane and Amelia went rigid with shock.

How was she tracking them?

Mackenzie provided them with a clue with her next statement. "My data is freezing up, but they're somewhere in this circle."

Her data? What did Mackenzie's data have to do with finding Sloane and Amelia?

And how did she know they were hiding nearby?

Suddenly, Sloane knew.

She slapped her face. "My phone! Remember when she returned my phone to me? She must have sent a request to track me and approved it on my phone before she gave it back!"

Unlocking her phone, Sloane opened up the Find Friends app. She hardly ever used it herself. Just when she was waiting for her grannies to pick her up and she wanted to know where they were. Sloane had only ever installed it on her phone to begin with because her dad had made her.

Yet there—along with her dad and her two grannies—was another name.

mackenzie snyder

can see your location

"Okay, I think my phone is reconnecting," Mackenzie said, around the corner and out on the main path. "It should get us within a few feet of her in a second."

"Oh no," Amelia whimpered. She pulled at her friend's arm, dragging her backward. "Sloane, we've got to go!"

"Hang on!" Frantically, Sloane swiped up on Mackenzie's name and tapped stop sharing my location.

Then she joined Amelia in booking it out of there.

They ran toward the fence, ducking and dodging behind and around trees and buildings to avoid the streetlights pouring down cones of golden light.

Behind them, Jayla Rychner cried, "Look! Over there!"

Risking a glance backward, Amelia saw four people running after them. Mac, the park manager, and two guards.

"Oh no!" she gasped.

"Don't look back!" Sloane warned through gritted teeth. Just like she had earlier in the week when she'd been trying to make it to home plate before the other team's softball, she focused everything she had on running.

Pumping as much power into her legs as she could.

Keeping her arms tucked close to her body.

Ignoring the stitch in her lungs.

Realizing that Amelia was falling behind.

Sloane slowed her pace and grabbed her friend by the arm. She looked around desperately for a place to hide. Amelia had many great qualities in a friend. Athletic ability was definitely not one of them.

But there was nowhere to hide.

They needed a plan. They needed to—

"Go this way!" Amelia cried. Without waiting for Sloane, she sped as fast as she could on her short legs, toward the chain-link fence around the park's edge.

"Wait—what?" Sloane gasped, dashing after her friend. "Amelia! We'll never make it over that fence in time!"

Jayla, Mackenzie, and their minions were gaining on them. They couldn't be more than a few yards behind them now.

"We've almost got them!" Mackenzie cried. "Get ready to get slayed, Sloane!"

Amelia, however, kept on running. With a speed and a determination unlike anything she'd ever shown before.

Because Amelia had spotted something no one else had.

Someone in a black unitard covered in turned-off LED lights.

Someone who wasn't used to there being anyone else on this side of the park.

Someone going up and over the chain-link fence.

Just like that person had done for the last couple of nights without getting caught.

If Amelia was going to get into trouble, she wasn't going alone.

With a shrill, primal scream, she launched herself at the intruder.

And crashed right into them.

Sixteen

THE GHOST OF MANIAC MCGEE

The person Amelia had caught tried to push her off. Amelia, however, dug her knees into their ribcage.

"Who are you?" she demanded, clawing at their hood. "Who are you?"

The person slapped and kicked at Amelia, but she refused to let go. As a shocked Jayla Rychner and her crew joined them, the intruder finally succeeded in pushing Amelia off.

Amelia, however, finally snagged her fingers into their mask and hood, yanking them free.

Blond curls fell out.

As Dr. Pickerington staggered to her feet!

"You!" Jayla Rychner gasped. "What are you doing?"

"She's your mystery ghost!" Amelia shook the mask at the history professor. "She's been breaking into Dr. Jamil's dig, disguised as Maniac McGee!"

"Is this true?" Shocked, the park manager turned to the professor for an answer.

The look on the historian's face was all the answer Jayla needed.

"See, I knew there wasn't a ghost," Devin said to Frankie. Who rolled her eyes and shook her head.

"Why?" the park manager demanded of Dr. Pickerington.

"Because I didn't want that horrible Dr. Jamil to say lies about my ancestors." Dr. Pickerington sulked.

All the Cedar Point employees looked more confused than ever. The professor crossed her arms and squeezed her mouth into a hard line. As though trying to physically transform herself into a clam with everything she knew trapped inside.

Sloane, however, was pretty sure she and Amelia knew what Dr. Pickerington was afraid of having revealed.

"Colonel Pike Pickerington made his money by cutting down the cedar trees on the peninsula and using them to build out-houses," Sloane explained.

"Luxury outhouses!" Dr. Pickerington exploded. "Not some cheap pine outhouses! Cedar is an expensive wood, you know! Er, I mean. If he had made his money that way. Which he didn't."

Jayla Rychner gaped at Dr. Pickerington like the historian had suddenly started babbling in French and the park manager couldn't understand a word of what she was saying.

Which, in all fairness, dressing like a ghost and ransacking an archaeological dig did seem like an extreme overreaction to the situation.

Frankie's face, however, suddenly lit up. "Oh! Does this have something to do with that sign Dr. Jamil's crew dug up? The one that read, Pickerington's Outhouses: for all the things you want to do out of the house? I didn't really get it, because I never want to use the bathroom outside the house. But I know that Clara, Trent, and AJ all thought it sounded really funny. Even Ryan was laugh-ing, and that guy never laughs at anything."

She kindly pulled up a picture on her phone and showed it to everyone.

The sign was old and very faded, but the message could still be easily seen.

As could the smiling face of someone who looked almost identical to Dr. Pickerington in her bonneted Victorian outfit.

"My great-great-great-great-grandmother!" The professor tried to snatch away Frankie's phone, but the guard was too quick for her. Angrily, the historian huffed, "No one respects their elders anymore! Outhouses were a perfectly respectable business back in the 1800s and early 1900s! I wasn't about to let him ruin their reputations!"

"By . . . telling the truth?" Amelia asked, confused.

"Oh, *the truth!*" Dr. Pickerington sneered. "Please! The truth is whatever you get enough people to believe."

The actual truth of the matter was, the historian had been caught trespassing on the Cedar Point property, as well as breaking into and vandalizing the archaeological dig. Devin and Frankie escorted her back to the front gate to wait for the Sandusky County Police to arrest her. While she probably wouldn't do jail time—just community service—for her mischief, it probably would be news.

With the picture of Pickerington's Outhouses included in every story.

Dr. Pickerington had done far more to draw attention to her family secret than Dr. Jamil ever could have done. Even if he had wanted to. A fact that seemed to be finally sinking in for her as Frankie led her off to the gate to meet the police.

"What about these two?" Mackenzie asked excitedly, pulling

out her phone so she could film Sloane and Amelia. "They're guilty of trespassing, breaking and entering, and vandalism, too! Just look at them!"

Sloane and Amelia looked at themselves. As Mackenzie had noticed, they were both still covered in brick and stone dust.

Plus, Sloane had a mallet in one hand.

Which was, admittedly, difficult to explain.

Amelia, however, had her friend's back. Before Jayla Rychner could say anything, Amelia spoke up. "And what about hacking into someone's phone by stealing their password? That's actually illegal, too. In fact, it's a federal crime. And I would know since my dad is a judge."

Mackenzie gasped in outrage. "How did I steal it? Everyone one the volleyball team knows that Sloane's password is slayer!"

"Oh, so you *admit* it?" Amelia crowed triumphantly.

"No!" Blushing furiously, Mac suddenly decided it was a good idea to stop recording the conversation and put her phone away.

"Really?" Amelia crossed her arms and cocked an eyebrow skeptically. "Because everything you do electronically leaves a record. We can find out when someone accepted your request to follow her. If it was during the time that you had Sloane's phone after she 'lost' it, then that's evidence that it was you."

"Her phone was already unlocked," Mackenzie sulked.

Jayla Rychner spoke up. "Even if it was, it's still illegal to make changes like that to someone else's device. Plus, if you really have been following Sloane around, that could break some anti-stalking laws too. Had I realized how you were tracking Sloane and Amelia without their knowledge, I never would have been okay with it."

By now, Mackenzie had gone from flushed in anger to green with anxiety.

Luckily for her, her Grandma Snyder came toddling toward them, led by Frankie, returning from handing Dr. Pickerington over to the police. She appeared far frailer than she had when she strutted into the Breakers Hotel with the dance team. In fact, she leaned on Frankie's arm as though one gust of the lake wind might sweep her out across the water like an empty Popsicle wrapper.

"Oh, thank you!" she wheezed, patting Frankie's arm. Then she collapsed against Mackenzie's arm as though unable to stand without help. "Come along, Mac. They can't question you without an adult present."

"You're an adult, and you're present," Jayla Rychner pointed out.

"Not anymore I'm not." With that, Grandma Snyder dragged Mackenzie away. The two of them headed in the direction of the Breakers Hotel. With Grandma Snyder getting sprier and sprier with every step she took farther away from them.

Jayla Rychner shook her head in disgust.

Sloane, however, slung her arm around Amelia and gave her shoulder a squeeze. "Hey, that's the first time you've ever stood up to Mackenzie. Well, stood up and won. Did you *see* her face?"

Realizing Sloane was right, Amelia smiled slowly.

"Yeah," she said, dazed. "I did."

Mackenzie had been the worst part of seventh grade for Amelia. Not only had she made fun of her constantly, she'd gotten other kids to do the same. Mostly, Amelia hadn't known what to do about it other than cry when she was by herself. On the rare occasion when she *did* try to stand up to Mackenzie, it had always backfired.

Leaving Amelia feeling more miserable than before.

But not this time.

This time, Amelia had stood up to Mackenzie—and *Mackenzie* had been the one to back down.

The one to walk away.

Something had shifted in the relationship between them.

Amelia was no longer someone Mac could reliably pick on to make herself feel superior.

Now Mackenzie knew that she risked being humiliated rather than embarrassing Amelia.

From now on, Mackenzie would hesitate before being mean to her.

While Amelia wouldn't hesitate to fight back.

Maybe they hadn't found Covington Collymore's lost time capsule. But at least Amelia had discovered more bravery inside herself than she'd realized she had.

It made for a dreamy walk through the darkened theme park, shadows and lights rippling together.

To Sloane and Amelia's enormous relief, Jayla Rychner wasn't mad at them anymore. Rather than taking them to the front gate to be arrested along with Dr. Pickerington, she thanked them for their help in catching the vandal.

Then she gave Amelia her phone back. Which was great!

Though, Jayla Rychner then immediately made Amelia call her family to let them know that she was all right.

Which was less great.

Amelia pulled up FaceTime, expecting to hear her family lecture her on being out so late. Before offering her suggestions on how they would have done it. Or—more likely, lately—smear strained smiles all across the camera while they held back all the things they really wanted to say.

Instead, they exploded with questions.

"Did we help?" Amanda Miller demanded as soon as her picture appeared. "Did we do that right?"

The Judge grabbed the phone from his wife and leaned into it like he thought he could crawl through it. "Or did we do it all wrong? Is that why you took so long calling us back? Did you think we did a terrible job of helping you, and you don't want to tell us that?"

Wait . . . what?

Her parents . . . wanted *her* approval?

That couldn't be right.

Yet it was. It took Amelia forever to assure her parents that they'd done a great job of assisting their daughter with her detective work. They still didn't look entirely convinced when the phone call was over.

But they did look proud of her.

Dazed, Amelia didn't know what to make of that as they waved goodbye to the park manager at the gate and headed back to the Breakers Hotel.

"I actually filmed when you talked to Dr. Pickerington." Sloane held up her phone for her friend to see. "If we come back and interview Dr. Jamil tomorrow to get his reaction, I think we might have something to put together for another video."

Amelia nodded, suddenly feeling a little less satisfied with the evening. Yes, they'd be able to put together something—but they hadn't found Covington Collymore's time capsule. Which also meant they wouldn't get the ten-thousand-dollar reward that he was offering.

Plus, how many followers would they lose?

Would BuzzFeed be one of them?

Pulling her phone out, Amelia checked their social media accounts. She let out a strangled gasp.

"Slo—" She couldn't quite get her friend's name out.

"Hm?" Sloane yawned and stretched as they reached the hotel's front lobby.

Unable to either talk or breathe, Amelia shoved her phone in front of Sloane's nose.

Sloane blinked, squinted, and focused her very tired eyes. The numbers in front of her didn't make any sense. She blinked, squinted, and focused again. When that still didn't work, she tried rubbing her eyes to clear them.

The number in front of her didn't change.

It remained 1,001,234.

One million one thousand two hundred thirty-four?

They now had over a million followers.

All waiting breathlessly for them to solve the case.

A case they probably couldn't solve.

Seventeen

The Reason "Why" Matters After All

"Oh-my-gosh-oh-my-gosh-oh-my-gosh-oh-my-gosh-oh-my-gosh!" Amelia hyperventilated into a plastic Cedar Point bag that had held a souvenir magnet and bracelet until a moment before when she'd dumped them out onto the bedroom floor.

They were back in the hotel suite, having just taken the elevator upstairs. They had run inside, panicking and slamming the door shut like a million people were quite literally following them.

Then Amelia collapsed on the floor.

"J-just breathe, Amelia," Sloane encouraged. However, her voice wasn't exactly steady either. Since her hair was done, she had snatched up a random strand of it and twisted it around the tip of her finger so tightly that her skin quickly went bone-white from the lack of blood flow.

Yet Sloane kept right on twisting her hair round and round it.

She couldn't stop.

"A million followers, Sloane!" Amelia wheezed, pulling her face up out of the bag. "What are we going to do?"

Sloane didn't know. She'd never had a million pairs of eyes on her before. A million! She might be known for her steady nerves on the volleyball court and the softball field, but she'd only ever had a couple of dozen people watching her there.

If she made a mistake, so what? It was just a couple of dozen people.

Now, if she and Amelia didn't figure this thing out soon, it would be in front of *a million people.*

All around the world.

People would literally be talking about what a disappointment they were in something, like, twenty different languages.

Releasing her hair, Sloane snatched the plastic souvenir bag out of Amelia's hands and began to hyperventilate into it too.

Granny Kitty and Granny Pearl came out of their room.

"What's going on out here?" Granny Kitty demanded in bewilderment. She wore a pair of flannel pajamas patterned with cartoon running shoes. Next to her, Granny Pearl's pajamas were covered in flowers and gardening tools.

"We're having panic attacks!" Amelia gasped.

Pulling her head out of the bag, Sloane explained the great news that they now had a million followers. And the less-great news that they were probably about to lose most of them.

The grannies listened sympathetically.

Then, when Sloane finally sniffled out the last details, they ordered hot chocolate. With extra marshmallows and whipped cream, plus a great big plate of warm cookies from room service. They plied Sloane and Amelia with these until both girls found their spirits rising on a cozy wave of chocolate-and-sugar bliss.

"What a terrible situation to be in!" Granny Kitty sighed, pinching Sloane's cheek.

"Anyone would feel panicky about it," Granny Pearl agreed, giving Amelia's cheek the same treatment. Everyone took a sip from their mugs. Then Granny Pearl delicately asked, "Do you want our advice? Or do you just want us to listen?"

Sloane thought over Granny Pearl's offer. Then she turned to Amelia and said, "I think I need advice right now. What about you, Amelia?"

"Yes, I think I need some help too," Amelia admitted.

"Clear your minds of everything you've learned so far," Granny Kitty advised, pouring more hot chocolate into their cups. "Go back to the beginning and don't rule anything out."

Granny Pearl took out a pad of notebook paper and a pencil. "Of the buildings that are here, which ones were on the peninsula in 1915?"

"The Coliseum, the Pagoda Gift Shop, the Convention Center, and the Eerie Estate." Sloane ticked them off on her fingers.

Her granny wrote each one down as she said it. When Sloane didn't list any other buildings, Granny Pearl prodded, "You didn't mention this hotel. The Breakers was here then too."

"Yeah, but it's been remodeled so much that the time capsule would have been found a long time ago," Sloane objected, reaching for another cookie.

"Right now, we're not ruling anything out, remember?" Granny Kitty said. "Add the hotel to the list, Pearl."

If they weren't ruling anything out, then Amelia thought of another building. "The lighthouse was here in 1915, too. In fact, it was here for something, like, fifty years before that."

Until now, Sloane and Amelia hadn't really considered the lighthouse as being a likely place for the time capsule to be hidden. If Covington Collymore I thought the owners of Cedar Point had stolen his land, then the lighthouse had nothing to do with that. It wasn't actually part of the park, having been there long before the park existed. It had been built in the 1860s and would have actually helped Collymore see dangerous rocks as he smuggled prisoners from the Sandusky County Jail. It had helped keep him safe, even if the same couldn't be said of poor, clumsy Maniac McGee.

And yet—and yet—was the time capsule *really* about how Zistel, the founder of Cedar Point, had stolen Collymore's land?

Sloane and Amelia had already found proof that Collymore had willingly sold his land to Zistel.

Maybe whatever Collymore had to say in his time capsule, it had nothing to do with that.

Maybe that time capsule was filled with jewels or money after all!

In which case, Sloane and Amelia never should have ruled out the lighthouse.

"Let's take another look at that letter," Amelia suggested with excitement.

Pushing away the remains of their late-night snack, Sloane pulled out her school Chromebook. She used it to pull up a larger version of the picture she'd taken back when they met Collymore at the Red Rambler Coffee House in Wauseon.

All four of them leaned forward to read it again.

> *My Dearest Petunia,*
> *The events of 1875 have always weighed heavily upon my mind. Reverend Callender says that the truth will set me free. But I fear that truth cannot be known before my death. Like a*

ship on Lake Erie, I can feel myself sailing off into my final
sunset. I've hidden a box near the land from which I ran my
business. When it's found, all will know what really happened.
The corner stone on which all lies rest will show itself to be a
fake and crumble. Until then—"The great ships sail outward
and return, bending and bowing o'er the billowy swells."

    Your devoted husband,

    Covington

"'The great ships sail outward and return, bending and bowing o'er the billowy swells.'" Granny Pearl read.

"Yeah, pretty fancy language, huh?" Amelia grimaced. "People talked like that back then, you know. All flowery and fancy."

"Maybe, but that's a quote," Granny Pearl explained. "See, it has quote marks around it. That means Collymore was quoting someone else."

Sloane and Amelia looked at each other. Obviously, they'd learned about quote marks in their English classes over the years. Just this past year, Mr. Roth had harped on it endlessly, stressing the importance of both researching and properly quoting that research. Yet neither one of them had noticed those quote marks.

Or wondered why Collymore I was quoting someone else.

They just thought it was a weird, old-timey person talking in a weird, old-timey way.

"Sloane, Google that sentence!" Amelia jumped up and down in excitement.

Sloane did just that.

"It's . . . a poem," she gasped. "A poem by some guy called Henry

Wadsworth Longfellow. Called . . . Amelia, it's called . . ."

She couldn't get the words out.

"Yes, yes—what's it called, Sloane?" Amelia demanded, practically using the couch as a trampoline.

"It's called 'The Lighthouse.'"

By the time Sloane and Amelia made their discovery, it was almost two in the morning. In early July in northern Ohio, that meant dawn would break in about four hours. If they waited until then, they'd be able to clearly see the lighthouse and check its cornerstones. Both girls—and the grannies, too—still felt that the sentence "The corner stone on which all lies rest will show itself to be a fake and crumble" was definitely a clue that one of those cornerstones was a well-disguised fake.

The sensible thing to do, obviously, would be to wait until daylight.

Sensible or not, neither Sloane nor Amelia could wait that long.

Especially not after Sloane went into the bathroom to brush her teeth and pull her hair back into its usual ponytail. Only to discover two blue rosebushes sitting in the bathtub once again.

If Jayla Rychner got wind of what the grannies had been up to while she was focused on Sloane and Amelia, the park manager would probably feel less forgiving toward their various misadventures.

Even if she wasn't looking for the time capsule herself.

Which they still couldn't rule out.

Sloane shot out of the bathroom like the rosebushes had grown clown faces. "Amelia, we need to find that time capsule quickly!" Turning to her grannies, she added, "And you two need to put those bushes back right now!"

"Oh, we would!" Granny Kitty put on her sweet-little-old-lady act. "Only, won't you need our shovel to break open that fake cornerstone?"

Granny Pearl held up the shovel and batted her eyelashes at the two girls.

Which would it be?

Return the rosebushes or find the lost time capsule?

"Grrr!" Sloane snatched the shovel out of Granny Pearl's hands. "Fine! You know, grannies, I really do appreciate your help. But could you please try to commit fewer crimes while you're doing it?"

"We will if you will!" Granny Kitty gave them a little finger wave as Sloane and Amelia left.

They took the elevator back to the lobby, expecting to find it dead.

Which it was—mostly.

Mackenzie and Grandma Snyder stood at the front desk, with the elder Snyder shouting furiously at the poor night manager. The elevator doors had no more than opened when a horrible, disgusting, positively putrid smell smacked both Sloane and Amelia in the face.

"Blech!" Amelia gagged, pinching her nose and staggering backward. "What *is* that?"

What it turned out to be were several dead fish.

Which Mackenzie and Grandma Snyder had found stuffed under their mattresses.

Stinking up their entire hotel room.

"I demand an explanation!" Grandma Snyder pounded her fist against the desk. While Mackenzie sniffed her clothes and grimaced.

"Grandma," she whined. "I can't smell like rotting fish at the dance competition! No one will want to stand near me!"

Certain that the explanation for the dead fish absolutely-most-definitely involved Granny Kitty and Granny Pearl, Sloane and Amelia snickered. Then they tiptoed out of the lobby, counting on everyone being too busy with the fish problem to hear the swish of the sliding front doors as they left. This didn't quite work as Mackenzie turned and glared at them. She opened her mouth to say something—probably about the shovel in Sloane's hands.

Only to get another whiff of the fish stench.

She promptly clapped her hands over her mouth and ran from the lobby.

Feeling like things were finally going their way, Sloane and Amelia headed out into the night.

The lake's damp chill clung to the shadows. They followed the curve of the peninsula to the north and then to the west. The shore eased from sandy to pebbly to rocky, with the waves crashing against them. From the shore, it made a soothing sound, but Sloane couldn't imagine riding in Covington Collymore I's little rowboat. Not from Sandusky to the Cedar Point peninsula.

Let alone across Lake Erie to Canada.

The sidewalk they followed led them from the hotel through the log cabins that people could rent to go "camping" in. The little houses all lay silent and dark, slumbering. Still, enough streetlights lit the way to make their trip quick.

Finally, the gray stone building rose up before them. It looked more like a storybook cottage than a proper lighthouse to both Sloane and Amelia. It was neither round in shape nor particularly tall. Instead, the tower was squarish and barely stood above the chimney's jutting out of the sloping roof.

Sloane and Amelia exchanged a look.

Then, Sloane shrugged and said, "Well, here goes nothing."

They first checked the corner on the front-right side of the lighthouse, tapping each stone and listening carefully. If any of them were hollow, they all sounded identical: *clunk-clunk-clunk.*

Moving to the corner to the left, they tried again.

Clunk-clunk-clunk.

Excitement seeping out of them with each dull "clunk," they moved to the back of the lighthouse.

Clunk-clunk-clunk.

Nothing! Sloane almost threw down the shovel in disappointment. They'd been so sure that this was it. Were they wrong—or did they just not know how to check for a hollow space?

They went to the last corner.

Sloane took a deep breath and tapped the tip of the shovel against the weathered stone.

Clunk-clunk-CLINK!

Clink? Clink!

"Did you hear that?" Sloane gasped.

"I heard it! I heard it!" Amelia cried excitedly, clapping her hands to her face.

Sloane knocked the shovel against the stone again.

Again, it clinked!

Certain, now, that they'd found the time capsule's hiding spot, Sloane hit the stone harder.

It cracked and buckled, dust rising up into the air.

She whacked it again, and the stone collapsed inward.

Revealing the empty space within.

Amelia shone her phone's flashlight inside, waving away a cloud of powdered stone as she did so. "There's a piece of paper."

Carefully, she pulled it out.

The paper felt thin and fragile to the touch. Almost like tracing paper, but yellowed with time.

"I guess this was all about a land deed after all." Sloane felt disappointed. Land deeds weren't nearly as exciting as lost money or missing gems. Even if Covington Collymore was going to pay them ten thousand dollars for finding it.

"It's not!" Amelia trained her flashlight onto the paper. "It's a letter!"

It was written in the same splotchy, spidery handwriting as the other letter by Covington Collymore I.

To whom it may concern, this is a full confession of my crimes. I, Covington Collymore I, did help many men escape from the Sandusky County Jail. Moreover, I charged them large sums of money for this. I did further steal all the valuables placed in every coffin I was to bury. However, the worst of my crimes occurred on the night of March 30, 1875 when I helped Murdock McGee escape from prison. He promised to pay me out of the million dollars within his trunks at the train station. Instead, I brought him out into the bay and pushed him over the side of the boat. Whether he drowned or swam his way ashore, I cannot say. But he was never seen again, and I took both his trunks and the money inside as my own. I did this for my family's benefit. The Reverend Callender says that I need to make a full confession to the authorities if I wish to go to heaven. He failed to say which authorities or when. I confess these crimes, knowing that one day, some authorities somewhere will find out. I can now die, knowing I shall go to my great reward in the sky.

"He was a murderer!" Sloane clapped a hand to her head, not quite able to believe it. "And—and—and a scam artist! Who thinks that this technically counts as 'confessing' what he did to the police?"

Dazed, Amelia said, "He murdered Maniac McGee. That poor guy didn't fall out of the boat. He was pushed. Covington Collymore the Sixth is *not* going to be happy about this."

"Oh, I already knew," a voice behind them said.

Whirling around, Sloane and Amelia discovered Collymore VI looming over them.

Amelia was right.

He didn't look at all happy.

Eighteen

Running Out of Tracks

Sloane and Amelia had been so focused on their discovery that they hadn't heard Covington Collymore creeping up on them. The dew-dampened grass had hushed his footsteps. Now he picked up the shovel that Sloane had dropped.

Not liking the looks of this at all, Sloane and Amelia got warily to their feet.

Up until now, Collymore had just seemed like someone's dad. True, a dad to an awful someone like CeeCee. But a dad just the same.

He still wore his dad khaki shorts with a dad T-shirt.

Collymore even had a broad dad grin on his face.

But it didn't look the least bit friendly.

"You see, my great-great-great-grammy knew exactly what my great-great-great-grampy had done. Talked in his sleep. A lot." As *he* talked, Collymore tested the weight of the shovel. The same way Sloane tested the weight of a baseball bat before swinging it. "So, when she got that letter, she knew exactly what her husband was talking about. She just about died of a heart attack on the spot, I'm told. If word got out about what he had done, the family's reputation would have been ruined. Worse still, McGee's family could have taken the Collymores to court to get their money back. So, she told her son. And he told his son—and so on."

Amelia flattened herself against the cold stones of the lighthouse, keeping both eyes on the shovel. She tried to decide whether or not she'd be able to duck in time, if he swung it.

The answer was "probably not."

"Then why send us to find it?" Amelia asked, stuffing her hands into her pockets and feeling for her phone. It had been recording ever since they'd heard that first "clunk" and knew they'd found the hollowed-out cornerstone.

Collymore shrugged. "For the past hundred years, every time Cedar Point tears down an old roller coaster or builds a new one, my family has been worried sick that we were about to lose our fortune. That the time capsule would be dug up, and the truth about Maniac McGee would be revealed. If I'd known it was safely hidden in this lighthouse, I never would have bothered hiring you two. But I thought it had to be over by the Coliseum for sure, and that was right where they were digging."

"We won't post anymore videos on YouTube," Sloane promised, keeping her eyes firmly on Collymore's legs. When she saw him brace them, she'd know he was getting ready to swing.

Amelia nodded, still fumbling with her phone. She was trying to turn the camera off and make an emergency phone call to 911.

To let them know that they were probably going to end up as dead as poor Maniac McGee.

Collymore laughed dismissively. "What do I care? You're just a couple of kids. Who's going to listen to you? Especially if you accidentally slipped and fell into the lake, just like Maniac McGee."

The grin faded from Collymore's face.

He braced his legs.

It was the signal Sloane had been waiting for. She grabbed Amelia by the hand and ran.

The metal base of the shovel whistled over Amelia's curls as Sloane jerked her away. The blade smashed against the stone lighthouse, tearing off a chunk of it.

Behind Sloane and Amelia, Collymore let out a furious roar. It sent chills down Amelia's spine as Sloane let go of her hand so they could both run faster. They fled out into the night, Amelia's feet pounding faster than she ever thought they could move. Risking a glance over her shoulder, she saw him following them.

Shovel still raised.

Ready to pound them into the pavement.

"Help!" Amelia tried to cry, but she was running so hard that it only came out as a dry whimper.

"HELP!" Sloane shouted it louder, but the wind caught the word and flung it out across the darkened lake.

They tried to angle themselves back toward the hotel. However, in their desperation to get away from their attacker, Sloane and Amelia had gotten turned around. They'd run the wrong way around the lighthouse and were now lost in a maze of the camping cabins.

Sloane ran up onto one of the porches—no more than a small, wooden platform—and banged on the door. "Help! We're being chased!"

However, whoever was inside, must have been deep asleep. No one answered.

And then a shovel bed whizzed toward her head.

Sloane saw it just in time, flinching to the side so that it crashed against the door, shaking its frame.

Yet, still, no one came to rescue her and Amelia.

Whipping around, Sloane kicked Collymore in the stomach before he could swing again. He double over with a cry of pain.

Though he hung on to that shovel.

This time, Amelia grabbed Sloane by the hand and dragged her along. "We're never going to wake anyone up before he's knocked us both out!"

Then tossed them into Lake Erie, just like his ancestor had with Maniac McGee.

Turning them into nothing more than two more ghosts. Doomed to spend eternity with Kewpie dolls.

On they ran.

Collymore staggered to his feet, following them.

The row of cabins unraveled, leading to a parking lot thick with cars. Sloane and Amelia hunched over, putting their hands and feet onto the cold, hard asphalt. As they crouched, both Sloane and Amelia tried calling the grannies—or better still, 911—but they kept getting "No Service" instead of bars on their phones.

The park's chain-link fence rose up before them, roller coasters looming beyond with curves like the backs of sleeping dragons. Amelia pointed at it. "This way! There have to be guards in there!"

Up the fence, they went. It shook and clinked, alerting

Collymore to their presence. However, his shovel swished use-lessly against the wires as Sloane and Amelia reached the top. They swung their legs clear and dropped down on the other side.

"Ha!" Amelia smiled smugly.

Until Collymore threw down his shovel and began to climb too.

Turning around, they ran again.

Somewhere in the darkness, Sloane and Amelia became separated.

"Amelia?" Sloane whispered, afraid Collymore would hear her. "Where are you?"

Sloane was near the Master of Mayhem. Even only partly fin-ished, that first slope looked more like a mountain than a hill.

A mountain with Amelia standing at its foot, her phone and selfie-stick off to one side

Held there by Covington Collymore.

"Amelia!" Sloane cried.

As she watched, Collymore shoved her friend into one of the cars.

To Sloane, he shouted, "Bring me that confession—or I'll send your friend on the last roller-coaster ride of her life."

Sloane's eyes followed the direction of the Master of Mayhem's first hill.

It still wasn't finished.

Amelia would go up . . .

. . . but when she came down again, she'd fall off the tracks.

Plummeting to the earth below.

"Run, Sloane! He won't do it!" Amelia tried to wriggle out of the car.

Collymore stopped her, snapping her seat harness into place. "Oh, I most definitely will."

Slowly, Sloane walked toward him. Her feet crunched over the gravel of the construction site as she walked past a crane and a bulldozer. Stopping at the base of the platform, she pulled the letter out of her pocket. "You can have it. But you need to come here."

Laughing, Collymore pushed a lever.

The car Amelia was in jerked forward. She screeched and grabbed at the bar.

Collymore yanked the lever back again, and the car jerked to a halt. Amelia's red curls blew around her face.

Sloane gave in.

She walked up the steps and across the platform. The letter shook in her hand as Amelia yelled at her not to do it.

Reaching Collymore, Sloane said, "Okay, you can have it, but—"

She never got to finish her sentence.

He snatched the letter from her hand and shoved her into the roller-coaster car next to Amelia. Sloane knocked her head against the metal harness, dazing her.

Preventing her from freeing herself before Collymore threw the lever again.

Sending them up the hill.

And toward their doom.

Nineteen

AMELIA'S SUPER POWER

Beneath the sparkling stars, the roller-coaster car lurched forward.

Up the half-finished track and toward the one-hundred-and-fifty-foot drop on the other side.

Without the rest of the track to catch it.

Amelia jabbed at the release button on her harness, but nothing happened. If they could just get out of the car before it started going too quickly, they'd be able to climb over the back and onto the tracks. "My harness is jammed!"

"Mine too!" Sloane cried as the car shivered. Since the electricity was only turned on for test purposes while the Master of Mayhem was being built, the roller coaster didn't seem to be working exactly as intended.

Rather than increasing its speed, the car's wheels ground against the track, reluctant to begin its trip upward.

Which Amelia could understand.

She was reluctant to begin it, too.

And even more reluctant to finish it.

Roller coasters—she'd always known they were a bad idea. Fling people up toward the sky and then smash them back to Earth again? Then be pleasantly surprised when they didn't end up as gooey messes?

This was why she never wanted to ride one.

Amelia had always known that, eventually, something would go wrong.

She just had never imagined that it would be someone actually trying to murder her.

Next to Amelia, Sloane twisted and contorted her body, trying to wriggle free from the harness. However, test car or not, the harness had been designed to keep people from getting out.

No matter how badly they wanted to do just that.

As Sloane continued to struggle, the car chugged along its tracks. It had only gone a little way, the climb being a lot slower than the downward fall. Amelia's heart skipped a beat.

Icy cold panic gripped her.

This was a nightmare.

She'd had *actual nightmares about this exact thing*!

That was it.

There was no way Amelia's brain was going to let the outside world be as scary as the things inside it sometimes were!

"Nopenopenopenopenope!" Amelia shrieked, twisting and contorting her body like a snake.

Harnesses are designed to keep people restrained, no matter what the laws of gravity and physics throw at them.

They are not, apparently, designed to restrain an extremely frantic, extremely determined Amelia.

Writhing, she got her head under one strap, and then tugged the rest of her body free as the car angled towards the starry sky.

Clutching the back of the car, she slid over it and onto the track, tumbling down the hill.

"Amelia! Help!" Sloane yelled. She tried to turn around, but her own harness kept her firmly in place. Darn her strong bones and muscles!

Left alone in the roller-coaster car, Sloane faced forward again.

She could see where the tracks gave way to the night sky.

To nothing but empty air.

This couldn't be happening.

This couldn't be how her summer vacation ended.

Best-case scenario, she was going to end up in a full body cast in the hospital rather than starting her eighth grade year with everyone else.

Worst-case scenario . . .

Well, Sloane didn't want to think about the worst-case scenario.

How had they gotten here?

Why had they ever accepted this investigation in the first place?

The end of the tracks loomed closer . . .

. . . and closer.

Sloane thrashed about wildly. This was it. This was—this was—

This was her jerking to a halt?

She flopped against the harness, her ponytail swinging around to smack her in the face.

Then the car began to chug slowly, *back* down the track.

The jagged ends of the Master of Mayhem moved farther and farther away, causing Sloane to sag against her seat in relief.

The car came to rest next to the platform where it had started. Amelia clutched the forward/reverse lever in both hands as though afraid that the car would head back up the hill again if she let go.

"Amelia!" Sloane still couldn't get out of her broken harness. "Help me out of this thing!"

"I can't," Amelia whispered, eyes big. "I'm trying to let go of the lever, but my fingers just won't do it."

Eventually—as her brain fully accepted the fact that Sloane wasn't about to end up as a patched-together gooey mess—Amelia tore her fingers free. Working together, they finally managed to squeeze Sloane out and around the straps of her jammed harness. Her feet gratefully hit the metal platform surrounding the Master of Mayhem.

She enveloped Amelia in a ferocious hug. "Amelia! You saved me!"

Still looking more than a little stunned, Amelia pointed over to where her phone was propped up on its selfie stick. "I think I even managed to film most of it."

"Wait—you stopped to turn on your camera before you saved me?" Sloane suddenly felt just the tiniest bit less grateful.

However, Amelia shook her head. "No, I dropped it there when Collymore grabbed me and dragged me up here. That guy is the worst. We have got to come up with a better review process before we let people hire us."

"Yes, he is definitely the worst," Sloane agreed grimly. "Let's go grab some pointy things from the construction site and see if we can find him."

They ran down the steps and through the construction site. Unfortunately, all the tools were locked up in much stronger boxes and lockers than at the archaeological dig. Unless they felt like trying to steal a backhoe, it looked like they weren't going to be able to get their hands on any kind of weapon. (Admittedly, the grannies would probably have stolen the backhoe. But then, they knew how to drive.)

Taking off, they ran for the exit, desperate to catch Collymore—even if they didn't know what they'd do with him once they did.

As it turned out, they didn't need to have a plan.

Because the grannies and the Seife kids had already caught Covington Collymore.

Sloane and Amelia screeched to a halt, gaping in surprise. Collymore lay on the ground, tied up with yarn. Brighton had his foot on Collymore as the backstabbing double-crosser snarled up at the boy. Not liking his attitude toward her brother, Skye brandished a knitting needle in the general direction of his nostrils.

"Behave or I'll set Bertram Cordelia on you!" the little girl threatened.

However, it was Brighton who was truly terrifying. He held nothing but a ball of yarn in his hands, but he yelled, "You leave Sloane alone! She's my almost-family, and you're not taking her away from me! Do you hear me? *You aren't taking my family away from me!*"

Collymore stopped trying to strain his way out of the yarn he'd been knitted into.

Definitely afraid of Brighton, Skye, and whatever they and the grannies were planning on doing next. (Possibly involving a concrete lawn ornament ending up someplace extremely uncomfortable.)

"Sloane! Amelia!" the grannies cried in relief. They enveloped both girls into ferocious hugs.

Granny Kitty added, "We heard one of the roller coasters running and assumed the worst!"

It was only then that Sloane and Amelia noticed Mackenzie and Grandma Snyder standing sourly over a very bedraggled, absolutely furious CeeCee. Who was pouting on the ground with her arms crossed.

"What are *you* doing here?" Sloane demanded. Before Mac could answer, Sloane added, "Hey, Skye—can I have one of those knitting needles?"

Clearly afraid—and correctly so—of where Sloane might be thinking about shoving that knitting needle—Granny Pearl hastily stepped in. "No, Sloane-y! Mackenzie was the one who warned us that Covington Collymore was up to no good!"

As it turned out, CeeCee had convinced Mackenzie to swipe Sloane's phone so she could accept the tracking request from Mackenzie through the Find Friends app. Then, the two girls followed Sloane's and Amelia's every movement, causing trouble whenever possible. Mackenzie thought it was all a prank so they could post embarrassing videos of the two detectives. What she didn't realize was that sneaky CeeCee was also texting the information to her dad so that Covington Collymore could swoop in and steal the letter if they found the time capsule. When Mac saw Sloane and Amelia slip out of the hotel lobby earlier in the night, she ran to tell CeeCee. Figuring that the two girls had something to do with the fish stink in the Snyder hotel room, Mac wanted revenge. However, when she told CeeCee what was going on, CeeCee promptly ran to tell her dad. Not because she was worried about Sloane and Amelia's safety.

Because her dad had dastardly plans for the two young detectives.

Suspicious and worried that something truly terrible was about to happen to Sloane and Amelia, Mackenzie found Grandma Snyder and told her everything that was going on. While Grandma Snyder was totally down with pranking Osburn and Miller-Poe Investigations—and the grannies along with it—she drew a line at anyone getting physically hurt.

So, she ran to the grannies . . .

. . . who grabbed the Seife kids . . .

. . . and together, everyone came to rescue Sloane and Amelia.

Tackling Covington and CeeCee Collymore along the way.

(Actually, Mackenzie was the only one who tackled CeeCee. With the result being CeeCee's athletic suit now had a *lot* less sequins and glitter on it. Plus, her hair bow was now missing and probably floating somewhere out in Lake Erie. Mac and CeeCee were no longer friends, with CeeCee now understanding why Mackenzie's nickname was Mac Attack.)

"You two are the worst and the biggest weirdos I've ever seen," Mackenzie snarked, crossing her arms sulkily. "And I don't get why everyone seems to want to watch your loser videos. But . . . I don't want to see either one of you in the hospital or anything like that. Besides, the volleyball team needs Sloane next year if we're going to massacre the other teams."

"Wow." Amelia blinked at her. "That makes me feel really warm and fuzzy inside."

Right about then, blue and red lights filled the parking lot outside the exit. Jayla Rychner came running—once more—with her security team flanking her and the police flanking them. Even Dr. Jamil appeared from the dig site, lots of old papers still clutched in his hands.

Everyone screeched to a halt at the sight of Covington Collymore knitted together on the ground. Held there by the Seife kids.

Sloane and Amelia explained what had happened as the police hefted Collymore up and exchanged the yarn for handcuffs. As Amelia filmed it, Sloane pulled the letter out of his pocket. "You see, he was determined to hide the proof that the first Covington Collymore was a liar, a thief, *and* a murderer. He thought he could rely on us to find the missing letter, and then force us to hand it over to him."

"Now that the truth is out, if Maniac McGee has any great-great-great-grandkids or whatever, they can sue the Collymores for the money his family stole." Amelia turned her phone around so she could talk into it.

"HA! Good luck finding them." Covington Collymore sneered. He managed to seem awfully cocky for someone in handcuffs.

"Oh, I'd be more than happy to set Ryan from my team on that," Dr. Jamil said, stepping forward. "There is nothing Ryan loves more than sifting through boring historical details."

Collymore wilted. To Sloane and Amelia, he bitterly complained, "You. This is all your fault. My family has always been so sure the time capsule had to be buried near the Coliseum. After all, it was one of the most impressive buildings in the park at that time! Why would he hide it inside some boring lighthouse, anyhow?"

No one would ever know the answer to that question, of course.

However, Amelia pointed out, "Maybe because the lighthouse was the last thing Maniac McGee probably saw before Covington Collymore the First pushed him overboard."

Undaunted, Covington Collymore VI kept trying to spin the past into a story he liked better. As the cops dragged him away, he yelled, "That doesn't prove murder! My great-great-great-grandfather probably thought he could swim! None of this means it wasn't all an accident!"

CeeCee ran after him, crying and demanding to know how she was going to fix the sequins on her athletic suit if he was in prison. Mackenzie and Grandma Snyder left too, both of them having cheered up quite a bit once they decided that it would now be easier for Mac to make herself the star of the We Dance Better Than U team. CeeCee having been her main competition.

Dr. Jamil didn't seem to mind having been roused out of bed, either. In fact, he seemed positively perky as he headed back toward the dig, chuckling as he went, "I'm so glad I came out here tonight after I heard about Dr. Pickerington breaking into my office. On top of everything, just think how mad she'll be when she hears that another of the town's founding fathers was a thief and a murderer!"

It was time for Osburn and Miller-Poe Investigations to return to their hotel suite. Paid for by the person they'd just had arrested. Hopefully, he'd paid in advance.

However, before they went, Sloane had a favor to ask. "Er, Mrs. Rychner?"

"Hmm?" The park manager rubbed sleepily at her temples. She was wearing her pajamas-that-looked-like-a-suit again. The same ones that Amelia's mom owned. So Sloane assumed the manager was probably sleeping in her office again. That looked less suspicious now, and more like a woman who really needed a vacation.

"Could we, uh, turn on one other ride? The carousel? Just for a few minutes? I want to talk to Brighton."

Brighton appeared more startled by this request than Jayla. Who had the defeated air of someone tired of dealing with Osburns, Miller-Poes, Seifes, and all the nonsense that came with them. Apparently deciding that the fastest, easiest way to be rid of them was to turn on the carousel, she did just that.

With the flick of a switch, it lit up the night. Warm, golden, magical . . .

. . . and just the tiniest bit creepy.

"You know, Cedar Point is supposed to own some haunted carousel horses," Amelia told Skye as the two of them climbed up onto the platform. "But none of them are on this ride, unfortunately."

Both Amelia and Skye sighed with disappointment.

Sloane and Brighton chose horses on the other side of the circle. Old-timey music crackled out from the speakers as the ride lurched forward. Picking up a bit of speed as it spun round and round.

"Um, Brighton?" Sloane began awkwardly—then stopped. Ugh. She still didn't know what to say. There was a part of her that still wanted to yell, *At least YOU have your mom! Stop acting like you have anything to worry about.*

But, well, Sloane didn't think that part of her should do the talking right now.

Or . . . maybe it should.

It just shouldn't yell.

Rather than look at her, Brighton ran his fingers over his horse's wooden bridle. Screwing up her courage, Sloane said, "You know, sometimes I get jealous of you and Skye because you still have both of your parents. Maybe you don't get to see as much of your dad as you want, but you do get to see him sometimes. I mean, *most* of the time, that doesn't bother me. But sometimes it does, and it always surprises me, and then I don't know how to act."

The younger kid scowled at her. "I knew it! You don't want us around! And your dad is going to do what you want and leave our mom!"

"What? No!" Sloane kicked her own horse in frustration. That wasn't what she meant! "I'm saying this all wrong. What I'm trying to say is . . . it's okay if you feel like all this is too special and you can't trust it. It's okay if you're worried that my dad and your mom won't get married even though you really want them to. It's okay to feel like you can't trust me. It's okay to feel whatever you feel. Just know that I'll always try to be a big sister to you. I mean, I don't exactly know how to be a big sister. So, it'll probably mostly be me giving you tips on how to swing a baseball bat or spike a volleyball or break into museums. But, you know. I'll try."

Brighton thought that over for a while as the carousel continued turning slowly through the night. They passed the grannies again and again, watching them eat from bags of cotton candy they had somehow convinced Jayla Rychner to get for them.

"What about Granny Kitty and Granny Pearl?" Brighton asked.

That was an easy one. Sloane nodded her head vigorously.

"Them too. Their best will probably involve either swindling you out of money or else helping them swindle someone else out of money. But they'll definitely do their best."

The seven-year-old had to think that one over for a bit too. Sloane let him, watching the darkened buildings of the causeway slowly spin past. Finally, Brighton spoke.

"Sloane, do you think you'd help me catch Poké Balls on the way back to the hotel?"

That was an easy one too.

"Sure, Brighton. In fact, anytime you need help catching Poké Balls, I'll be there for you."

Brighton smiled.

Far behind them, Amelia and Skye talked enthusiastically about ghosts.

Off to the side, the grannies ate their cotton candy.

Above them, the stars sparkled as they climbed off the carousel.

Everywhere Sloane looked, everything felt exactly as it should be.

Epilogue

Of course, things couldn't stay perfect forever. Once again, Jayla Rychner insisted that Sloane and Amelia FaceTime their parents and explain everything that had happened. Apparently, there were all sorts of forms David Osburn, Amanda Miller, and the Judge would need to sign. Promising that they wouldn't sue the park just because their daughters had almost died on one of their roller coasters. At the hands of a homicidal maniac.

Sloane and Amelia didn't see how any of that was the fault of Cedar Point. But, being the daughter of a judge, Amelia understood the importance of not being sued. It sounded dreadful. And even worse, *boring.*

"Boring" was something that Amelia avoided at all costs.

So—reluctantly—she took out her phone and called home while Sloane did the same.

Instead of Amelia's mom and dad, her half siblings answered.

"Amelia?" Ashley blinked into the camera in surprise. "Hey, Aiden! It's Amelia!"

She swiveled the camera so Amelia could see her brother doing upside-down crunches from some sort of medieval-looking contraption in the Miller-Poe's big, shiny basement. (On more than one occasion, Aiden had tried to explain what the metal torture thing was and how it was actually quite good for your health. But Amelia absolutely refused to listen.)

"Are Mom and Dad awake?" Amelia asked.

To her enormous relief, they were not. Figuring that Aiden and Ashley counted as adults since they were both in college, Amelia took a deep breath and told them everything. In conclusion, she added, "So, um, I guess maybe my clumsiness and extreme fear of roller coasters sort of works for me?"

She waited nervously . . .

. . . for the strained looks that meant Aiden and Ashley were holding back suggestions about how Amelia could have done things better. For the clenched teeth and puffed cheeks. For the fists clutched tight until the bones almost poked through. All to keep back an explosion of words.

Instead, Aiden and Ashley just exploded.

But . . . not with suggestions.

With cheers?

And—and praise?

That couldn't be right.

"Yeah, take *that,* Master of Mayhem!" For some reason, Aiden karate-kicked the medieval torture thingy. Which was weird, because he didn't know karate.

"And that, Collymore, you creep!" Ashley slammed her Pilates ball against the floor with so much force that it bounced up and tried to attack the exercise machine, too.

There followed all sorts of shouting, with Aiden and Ashley praising Amelia's intelligence and determination. While also promising to do all sorts of bloodthirsty things to both Covington

Collymore VI and the Master of Mayhem roller coaster as soon as they got a chance.

Aiden and Ashley were so noisy about it, that they woke up Amanda Miller and the Judge. Who came downstairs to demand to know what was going on.

When they found out, there were even more slightly terrifying compliments.

"That's my girl!" her mom crowed. "Pulverize that man! Smash his face into the ground!"

"But hide the evidence!" the Judge warned.

Taken aback, Amelia gasped, "I don't think I'm going to do either of those things, but . . . thank you? I think?"

Her family had always reminded Amelia of a pack of barbarians. Screaming, pillaging, physically overwhelming, possibly torch-carrying barbarians. But this was the first time she'd ever really thought of those barbarians as having her back.

Just like Granny Kitty and Granny Pearl had Sloane's back.

Yet when she'd asked for their help yesterday, they'd given it to her. No questions asked.

Again, just like Granny Kitty and Granny Pearl.

And right now, they were cheering on Amelia just like Sloane's family cheered at her softball and volleyball games.

Amelia had never before realized that the torches carried by barbarians could actually be quite warm and comforting.

Yet a blissful coziness surrounded her as she listened to her family whoop and attack the exercise equipment. That coziness carried her all the way back to the hotel and lulled her off to sleep even with Skye and Bertram Cordelia in bed with her.

In fact, Amelia was still smiling dreamily as they lugged all their stuff downstairs the next morning.

Smiling even though she and Sloane weren't getting paid for the case they'd solved.

For some strange reason, Covington Collymore VI didn't seem to think he owed them anything.

"I should have gotten a signed contract." Amelia sighed as they packed up the grannies' station wagon. "My parents always say, 'Make sure you get a signed contract.'"

"That comes up a lot?" Sloane asked.

"It does in my family."

At least the hotel suite and the platinum passes were already paid for. They could come back to Cedar Point as much as they wanted to for the rest of the year.

"The rest of your life, actually," Jayla Rychner said, having arrived to say goodbye. She'd exchanged her pajamas for her usual suit and heels. She looked shockingly put-together and professional, given how little sleep she'd had last night.

Smiling at Sloane and Amelia, she explained, "I've upgraded your passes to lifetime versions with all the add-ons like free parking and free meals. That's for your parents, too, when they bring you. As a way of saying 'thank you' for all the crimes you solved. And also, as a guarantee they won't sue us."

Sloane and Amelia shook her hand and smiled weakly.

Honestly, neither one of them was in a hurry to come back to Cedar Point.

Sloane was still afraid of clowns. Amelia was still afraid of dolls.

And now they both had a deep phobia of roller coasters.

"Hey, why were you at the park the last two nights?" Sloane asked. "We thought maybe you were looking for the missing time capsule."

Jayla Rychner blinked in surprise, and then laughed. "I wish! I've had so much to do that I've been sleeping in my office on the couch. There were a few—er—kinks that needed to be worked out in the design of the Master of Mayhem you were, uh, riding."

Rather than ask for more details, Sloane and Amelia quickly shook the hand of the park manager again, and got into the station wagon.

Only to leap back out again.

Two blue rosebushes were hidden on the floor.

"Don't be so obvious!" Granny Kitty hissed as Granny Pearl waved goodbye to Jayla Rychner. As soon as they were sure she'd gone, they grabbed the rosebushes and shoved them into the back end of the car. "I would think that, as private detectives, you'd know that snitches get stitches."

"It's not snitching to say 'Ow!' when you get attacked by thorns." Sloane rubbed at her ankle.

"A small price to pay!" Granny Pearl said innocently as she squeezed behind the wheel. "Buckle up, everyone!"

After Sloane did just that, Brighton handed her a packet of Hot Cheetos. He had his tablet out and asked, "Want to catch Poké Balls on the way home?"

Sloane grinned back at him. Weirdly, she felt like her mom was close by. Closer by than she had felt in a long time.

Maybe because Sloane knew that her mom would be proud of her for talking with Brighton.

For figuring out a way to change, but still stay herself.

Just like Amelia had done with her family.

Maybe they really would get a deal with BuzzFeed or Apple TV. The video Amelia had put together was already racking up the views.

But then again, maybe they wouldn't.

Either way, both Sloane and Amelia knew they both had people to count on.

They also knew they could count on themselves.

Whatever happened, they knew they could handle it.

Acknowledgments

Cedar Point Amusement Park is a real place, and it really was created by a German immigrant named Louis Zistel. The Coliseum, the Pagoda Gift Shop, the lighthouse, the Breakers Hotel, and several other buildings mentioned are real as well. Everything else is made up. Other than possibly Amelia's fear of roller coasters, which is actually my fear. Those things terrify me, and if you tried to make me ride one, I'd probably shoot right out of it just like Amelia.

Thank you to my childhood friends, Sheri Rychner and Monica Callender, for letting me steal their last names to use. Meanwhile, I have to make a correction to an error in the acknowledgments of my previous book, *Tangled Up in Nonsense*. The inspiration for Ma Yaklin's mansion was the Stranahan Mansion at Wildwood Metropark, not the Secor Mansion as I erroneously called it. They owned an entirely different mansion. It's tough being a millionaire.

Thank you to my agent, Hilary Harwell, for everything she's done to bring the Tangled Up in Luck series to the world. Additional thanks my fantastic editor, Kate Prosswimmer, for her excellent eye and guidance. Thank you to Nicole Fiorica for assisting her in that process and to Flavia Sorrentino, the cover artist. Flavia's artwork is so gorgeous, it always makes me swoon when I see what she's designed.

Without the continued support of my husband, daughter, parents, and sisters, I would never be able to write as much as I have. Their encouragement has provided much-needed boosts of confidence over the years! I couldn't have done it without any of you!